ASSASSINATION ATTEMPT!

Alone Wolfe

The Author

I0590980

ROBERT WORKMAN

Direct Media Marketing, Inc.

www.robert-workman.com

Avalon's slow-motion approach down the rough stairway in a snatched mini dress paused time and space in the musty void that surrounded us. The international runway phenomenon looked like she stepped out of a glossy photo on Jack's Wall of Fame and onto the staircase before me.

Her slender ankles grew upward into a mannequin's perfect calves and curvaceous, long, three-point legs that climbed up to slim, bikini-friendly hips. The skin-tight pink fabric squeezed an anorexic waist that ascended into pronounced pointed breasts, and softly tanned bare shoulders that made you want to grasp them and pull her forward into your arms.

In the dim light, the limbal rings around her cobalt irises thinned as her pupils enlarged and, once again, she read my mind. She smiled. In her seductive accent she said, "I will remember to dress incognito less often. Oui?"

For Doug

THANKS

James Charles Kingsley Montgomery, Angie, Mike, Priscilla.

Cover Design by: King of Designer on Fiverr.

BOOKS BY ROBERT WORKMAN

FICTION

ASSASINATION ATTEMPT! *Alone Wolfe*
IMMIGRATION INVASION! *A Family Affair*
MAXIMUM PREJUDICE: *A Love Story*

NON-FICTION

Selling, The Most Dangerous Game
Hired Gun II – Blasting Business Politics
Hired Gun – You're #1, and Somebody Hates It

Table of Contents

1

Jack

* * *

I stepped out of my booth at the Metro Diner and onto Montgomery Street, snapped on my aviators. Seconds later, I unwound them off my ears. A minute after that, clipped them on again. I wished the sky would make up its mind; I had enough indecision swirling in mine.

Helios wrestled with overweight clouds during a morning of vacillant weather in Manhattan's Lower East Side. They both lost. Warm, humid winds mediated between rain-soaked city streets and sun-glazed sidewalks.

At a crosswalk, I paused and scrolled through my phone for a mental massage of the usual daily good news: alcohol, drugs, murder, rape, terrorism, theft, war. A sheriff's deputy was killed serving a warrant, a military weapons truck was hijacked, the audit of Fort Knox gold reserves was being stalled, and sestercentennial celebrations were in place for the Tall Ships and the Statue of Liberty.

The mizzle grew thicker as I walked. At East Broadway I popped my collar. My head was tilted down and I observed my boots as they splashed through shallow slicks on the pavements of Grand Street. Up ahead, sporadic precipitation from the heavens accumulated on a sign suspended above me by a cantilever: Jack's Gym.

The eponymous placard over the club's glass door was half a century old. Some of its lights still worked. Its overflow of drizzle flowed down and embellished the soft doeskin of my trench coat with chocolate brown spots.

The NYPD cruiser and meat wagon double-parked on the street behind me should have told me something. I should have observed, should have noticed. I was a P.I., a Delta op in my previous life. I didn't miss things, especially blatant conspicuous anomalies.

But my head wasn't in New York City. The nation's capital called; I was wanted at home. *Can I be in two cities at the same time?* Wedded life was new to me, six weeks. For reasons that perplexed many people, the world's wealthiest widow proposed to me after we survived a massive firefight. The lovely and seductive Electra White married me in the White House Rose Garden and I became stepdad to her two boys.

The tall slender Texan with auburn big hair and prominent cheekbones became friends with the First Lady as neighbors. While Pershing Park was under reconstruction, her deceased husband, Preston T. White, horse-traded for it with the federal government. He upstaged the White House directly across the street with the Greek Revival design of his new five-story White Mansion. In the opinions of Electra White and First Lady Yvonne Jackson it was only natural that POTUS and FLOTUS stood in our wedding party as Best Man and Matron of Honor.

I may have been walking the streets in lower Manhattan, but I was wanted in Washington, D.C. What I wanted was a cigarette. What I needed was the routine of a workout for my body's motions to realign the thoughts in my head.

I pushed the doorbell button, stood aside, waited. A few moments longer than usual, a buzzer sounded; the security latch clicked its release. The 27 steps up to the second level always seemed dark, even during daylight in summer. A dust-covered fluorescent light that burned out years ago held its place in its disinterested existence overhead.

A thousand times before, I'd made the creaking uphill trek. Traces of stale cigar smoke, aged for decades in the exposed wood floorboards and walls, greeted my senses. They blended with the scent of sweat equity from Jack's devotees who invested in their muscular development.

The boards of the wood staircase creaked beneath the burden of my 243 pounds as I ascended. I passed by staircase walls lined with photos and posters of Jack's celebrated alumni: Mr.

Olympia, IBC middleweight champ, Olympic shot putter, WWE tag team champs.

"Jack's Wall of Fame" was a personal project of mine. I posted the 8 x 10 glossies of the club's heroes for the gym's only owner and employee out of pride and respect. But Jack didn't care about celebrity, or about frou-frou amenities. He preferred before/after photos of his street-level clientele. Jack said he didn't *improve* the joint because the improvements he wanted to see were in his clients.

The rest of the gym adhered to the same theme of non-décor. Paint peeled from the walls, tired from decades of deliberate neglect. Several absent tiles in the pressed-tin ceiling left dark holes that exposed ancient wooden joists. The solitary source of refreshment was a watercooler, retired from the Greyhound Port Authority Bus Station decades ago.

As I climbed, I closed my eyes and inhaled the musty aroma that welcomed me back. When I opened them again, my peripheral vision only recognized the existence of the glossy pictures, not their details. What I noticed was—nothing.

There was no sound, no chatter. No weights crashed onto the splintered wooden floor. No soulful speedbag rhythms, no heavy bag groans and punches.

Except for the gentle rustle of rain-soaked outer wear and the muffled tones of men's conversations, the place was quiet. At the top of the stairs, I turned and looked into Jack's office through one of his internal windows.

The sight of the homicide lieutenant struck me as oddly out of place. I thought, *What's Happy doing here?*

A pedestal next to the railing held Jack's daily sign-in ledger. The date at the top of the page: Monday, June 29, 2026. I picked up the ballpoint pen on a chain taped to its side. When Jack tagged me with the nickname, Mister Potato Head, I answered back by making my signatures with a simple, illiterate, *X. So, why was my X already logged in ahead of me at 9:15 a.m. this morning?*

Lt. Ralph "Happy" Moynihan half-turned and looked over his shoulder. The cordial neighborhood detective greeted me, obviously hopeful for my crime scene input and expertise. "Oh, no," he said. "What the Hell are you doing here?"

"I live here," I said. "Almost. My pre-work workout. What's going on?"

Happy looked at his watch under an arched eyebrow. "Two guys, over there. Came in and found him like that, called it in."

I asked, "Him, who?"

Happy jerked his head toward the office door. The blood drained down to my feet. I felt empty, transfixed, didn't want to move. Somehow I stepped across, looked inside.

The old guy was seated in his green shop chair behind his antique partners desk. His upper torso stretched prostrate across it. His hands gripped the far edge of the leather inlaid mahogany as if he clung for his life. Semi-long white hair cascaded off his shoulders onto the opened books and binders beneath his chest.

I didn't want to believe what my eyes told me they saw. I knew who it was; knew damned well who it was. Jack was my mentor; Jack was my sensei; Jack was my friend.

Jack was dead.

2

Happy

* * *

Water ran down my clothes and pooled on the worn-out floorboards inside the disheveled office. My hands were jammed into my coat pockets and my absent-minded fingers scratched around for whatever they didn't find.

I stood in the office doorway and stared. That wasn't Jack; it couldn't be Jack. He may have been 86, but he was as healthy and strong as a man 30 years younger. My eyes couldn't turn from the sight of him, stretched face down across his desk. I didn't want to look, didn't want to see, but there he was, in front of me. It couldn't be. Jack. Dead.

My favorite place to receive his words of wisdom sat empty before him: a fifties postmodern western chair, green, with a bas-relief bucking bronco stitched into the thick vinyl seatback. There was only enough room for two people to sit beside his desk. The rest of the space was jammed with abandoned file cabinets, worn-out chairs, stacks of newspapers. Bookshelves behind him sagged under the weight of their heavy, dusty volumes.

I said to Happy, "So, what the Hell are *you* doing here?"

Hap stood 6' 2" with a flattop buzz cut and a Glock G20 short frame 9mm beneath his jacket. He nodded toward a couple of my gym friends a few feet away. "Those guys found him; didn't know how to report it. Looks like a heart attack."

Mike and Jesse stood off to the side, uncertain about what they should be doing. Happy added, "Unexplained death; we got here as soon as we could. I didn't want anyone contaminating the scene. Like you."

Lt. Ralph "Happy" Moynihan and I had more run ins than either of us liked. It was his cop buddies who christened him with the Happy moniker because he never seemed to be happy, and because his real name was Ralph.

"So, you knew him well?" he asked.

"Yeah, you could say that."

"Care to elaborate?"

I asked, "What have you got so far?"

"You're seeing it. Their call came in at ten; we're just around the corner." Happy raised his voice a notch and appealed to the crime scene technician who examined Jack's eyes and status of rigor mortis. "So, Ted, time of death?"

15

The guy who stood over Jack's body spoke without looking over. "Hour ago." If you didn't know where to look for it in the overcrowded office, you wouldn't have noticed it. The hands of the round Sinclair Oil clock that displayed its green dinosaur pointed to 10:30 a.m.

God, Jack. What the Hell happened? You never saw a doctor in your life; you never missed a day at the gym. You're the personification of health and strength. You're Jack.

I stepped toward Mike and Jesse, friends of mine across the years from working out in the gym. The pair of FDNY lifers sat on a couple of the gym's mismatched metalflake vinyl benches.

"I'm sorry you had to find him," I said.

Jesse hung his head. He couldn't speak. I liked Jesse. I turned to Mike. He grimaced a non-smile and nodded his head, weighted with sorrow.

"What can you tell me?" I asked.

Happy approached us. "Look, Wolfe, I know you and the guy were friends, but don't interfere with police business."

I didn't grimace. I didn't shoot him a mean stare. I just looked at Lt. Moynihan with the calmest, most detached non-expression I had in my repertoire. That made him nervous. "Scram," I said. "I'm talking to my friends."

Happy, wasn't. But he read my signals and made the wise decision to step aside. He said, "I don't get paid enough to deal with the likes of you."

"Maybe you should find another job," I said.

I didn't like the way he gave me a thorough once over. He replied, "Don't tempt me," and turned back to his crime scene team.

I turned back to Mike. "What gives?"

"I don't know," he said. "We came in when we got off our shift this morning. He was laying there, like that."

Jack opened six mornings a week at 8:00. I arrived with the regular crowd that matriculated later, around 10:00. The numbers grew through the day into the evening until he closed shop at 8:00 p.m.

I wanted to sit with him like I used to do, be with him like I used to be. But not like this. Not with a veteran crew of sober CSI professionals that inspected his office and his mortal remains, zipped him up in a plastic body bag, called it a day and stopped to drink things out of their minds with some rotgut at a watering hole before they went home from work.

I knew that was their job; but it wasn't mine. I wanted to be with Jack, his spirit. I looked up, stared through the ancient tin ceiling, had a feeling I already was. Both quarreling angels on

17

my opposite shoulders called a temporary cease-fire. They agreed: "Let's get out of here."

That was my last training session at Jack's. I felt uncomfortable. I wanted to clean out my locker, get out of there, go home, wherever the Hell that was.

I walked around the desk, behind my friend in his final seat. Out of habit, I leaned forward, took care not to scrape my back against his thumbtacked *objets d'art*. Curled from age and sunlight they hung, thumbtacked on the walls of the tight space: postcards, letters, photos with friends.

And magazine spreads: Jack's office became a minor gallery of major models. They checked in from seven continents and rented the landmark old-school inner-city sweatshop for glossy magazine photo shoots. On any given Saturday morning, the scenery inside Jack's Gym improved in dramatic fashion.

Scantily clad tanned and taut young beauties juxtaposed their smooth, lithe, bodies against the rough, raw, background décor. On many Saturday mornings, the resident magazine gatefolds posted on the walls of his inner chancery sparked adolescent conversations among us middle-aged men.

My mind refused to dwell on memories in that room, at least for the time being. The M.E. crew and Happy permitted me the courtesy of a final moment. I wanted to say goodbye, laid my hand on Jack's back one last time. A moment later, I said, "Happy, I'm glad you're here."

"I'm flattered," came his sarcastic reply. "Why?"

"Because if he died of a heart attack, it was induced." I grabbed Jack's black T-shirt at his waist and yanked it up over his shoulders.

"Hey!" said the lieutenant. "You can't!"

He stopped when he saw it: a red dot in the left side of Jack's back, behind his heart. There was no blood. The soft red puncture wound made the area around it feel hard at the source, then mushy around it.

Happy leaned forward for a closer look. His fingertips gently pressed the penetration trauma around the wound. "No hesitation marks," he said.

My eye roll was involuntary. "I don't think he poked around before he stabbed himself in the back, Happy."

The lieutenant ignored my comment. "Icepick," he said. "No laceration drainage."

I felt my body tense, my jaws tighten. "Shivved from behind," I said. "A pro. He used some kind of blood arrester to prevent bleeding." I drew in deep breaths through my nose because my jaws were clenched so tight it felt like my teeth would crack.

I said, "The CIA learned that trick from the Mafia. When they do an autopsy and he lies on his back, they often don't see the puncture wound that caused the alleged heart attack so that's how it goes down."

Happy said, "Old-school tactic meets old-school victim. Good M.O. Had to be somebody he knew. They shouldn't be hard to find. That register over there lists everyone who's been here today."

I said, "Sure, it does. It lists me, too, but I just got here. You think the killer signed in? Maybe he left his address and phone number, too, just to be helpful. Come on, Ralph. You're better than that."

Happy's eyes squinted. He ground his teeth. "I don't like you, Wolfe. Never have. I don't like your cowboy attitude; I don't like that ridiculous arsenal you carry, and I don't like how the White House covers for you."

He got so wound up he had difficulty finding his words. "You're a mediocre P.I. God knows how you got your license. And now you've become some kind of media darling. You've got to be the luckiest son-of-a-bitch alive."

"Somebody up there likes me," I said.

"It's no ancestor of mine," he said beneath his breath.

Then he detonated again. "Screw you! You back into things; they fall into your lap, and you come out a hero. How the Hell you married into that White fortune, so you live ... wait a minute. What *are* you doing here? Aren't you supposed to be in Washington?"

One of the CSI team nudged Happy. He scribbled his signature on a form. Without looking up he asked, "Aren't you supposed to be at the White House today?"

"Tomorrow," I said. Then, "Maybe."

"What do you mean, 'maybe?'"

Minutes before, when I stood beneath the rain rivulets outside, my capacity for decisions was overloaded with ponderous questions. This dropped a piano on top of them. I looked at Jack's body across his desk. "Something came up," I said.

3

Cody

The disgruntled lieutenant backed away, bumped into one of the forensics crew. With an involuntary protest, Happy thrust his hand forward. He almost knocked some junk off of Jack's desk. Jack had a lot of junk on his desk.

"Oh, no!" he said. "You're not getting involved. Homicide is my jurisdiction; this is my case. I don't want you anywhere near this." He paused, then muttered under his breath: "Hell, our morgue couldn't handle the volume."

The abrupt dichotomy between my thoughts and feelings reminded me of my deployments. On the outside I was as clear and detached as if I floated 50 feet above and looked down. Inside, my guts roiled with violent waves of anger. Inside, I cried with grief within a raging tempest of emotions.

Delta Force training at Fort Bragg JSOC instilled thoughts and practices so deeply into the creases of my brain that they would never go away. It was a grim realization, but I was used to it. I was going in on this one, and I was going in alone.

I thought about the butcher that stabbed an icepick into the heart of a man who was all heart. Literally, stabbed in the back. My hands balled up inside my pockets. My fingernails told me they needed a trim when they bit into the flesh of my palms. I said, "Ralph, I just pushed my chips into the middle."

As I said the words, a clear thought hit me. *Why am I able to think so clearly?* I walked into the murder of a close friend amid impending foul weather and ... *nothing*. I should have felt a lot worse. It didn't fit.

My Sunday school teachers cautioned me, "Vengeance is mine, sayeth the Lord." But I knew something they didn't. God's a busy guy; so, He sub-contracts. That's where I come in.

Don't get me wrong–I'm not crazy. I don't claim to talk to God. I mean, come on, who talks to God, really? But I do receive His messages. They aren't subtle. And when something gets to the point where He puts my chess piece into play on the board of Fate, it means He's Really Pissed.

In certain supremely evil cases, God assigns His vengeance to be delivered on terra firma by proxy. He grants His forgiveness, but when the assignment comes to me, it means He wants plaza-street-level consequences. That's where I pick up my Command Contracts to serve as a pro bono avenging angel, incarnate.

The case was surrounded by all the telltales of the living Hell that foretold every assignment sent to me from above. A tragedy so close to home, manic barometric pressure, an advancing storm front and severe weather flare up. There was no mistaking the delivery of my Divine messages. When I received heavenly directives to serve as an earthbound proxy of justice, those foreboding conditions made me feel like I swallowed an earthquake.

When the telltale factors combined they made me wish I only walked through a storm instead of ingesting it. My head felt like it was going to explode, my insides roiled like a storm at sea. They told me that something powerful and deadly lay ahead of me. And they came from a higher power.

Where were they?

The problem was, I felt fine. My mind was lucid. I didn't have to lose my breakfast. The only thing I wanted was a smoke. *What's the matter?*

It was time to apply Logic 301. *If a coming challenge is supremely perilous, if I receive an advance warning from Above that assaults my physical, mental and spiritual health, it's always a forewarning of an extremely difficult and life threatening challenge. And until I get involved, the portents make me feel like I'm about to come apart at the seams.*

But I don't feel that way at all. So, this must be an easy one, right? I'm not pulling down the pillars of any Temples; I'm not saving the world. It'll be a nice change of pace. I'm just solving a murder.

It became obvious that this undertaking was not Heaven sent. It emanated from the dog pit of the city streets. I racked my focus onto one subject: Jack's killer. "Single Layer Thinking," I believe they called it. I called it opening a can of WhoopAss.

The F22 Raptor that sky hooked my emotions blasted ballistic through all four stages of psychological Shock. Anger and Rejection flashed past and I levelled off at Acceptance. The Acceptance I embraced was simple. I accepted the fact that I was going to nail the son-of-a-bitch that killed Jack.

Happy read my face. His was flushed. "Damn it, Wolfe! I don't need this! You ran me out on Pier 16 on decommissioned ships, in January, in the freezing rain, to find four of your victims. All dead, of course."

"Four of my attackers," I reminded him.

"And the last time! The last time, my forensics guys laughed me out of the autopsy suite! The prime evidence I delivered was a hand and a foot because your cat made dinner of the rest of him."

My exasperation was evident in my voice. "It was inside our home, a pair of hired killers. They picked the wrong studio when they tried to kill my sister. That's why we have our guard dog." I paused. "I don't give a damn, Happy. I'm going to nail this bastard."

"You're not going to nail anyone. Because you're not going to *do* anything. And a mountain lion is not a damn guard dog!"

"He is in our house. And his name is Cody. He gave up enough for you to make a positive ID. Besides," I said, "You got your vital data from the second guy."

Happy's voice carried residual anger still in place from over a year ago. "Barely! You call that mess your sister left us, a *guy?* What is it with your family and houseguests? We're used to seeing victims of gunshot wounds, but not 50 hollow points from a Tommy Gun at close range."

I said, "She's an artist."

I needed a smoke. Damn, I needed a smoke. I felt in my pockets, found my crumpled pack of Marlboro Reds. I thumbed the wheel of the Zippo my grandfather carried through his WWII POW camp. Its blue and orange flame licked the end of the cigarette.

Smoke, good; palate, dry. I need a drink. It's 10:45 in the morning, and I need a drink. Hell, I need a double.

Happy protested. "The Medical Museum in Silver Spring, Maryland put the autopsy photos on display. They called us the next day. They had to pull them down. Tourists were puking!"

"They were hired assassins," I said. "They lost." I turned toward the lockers in the back. "I'm grabbing my gear."

In the back of the gym, I slid a threadbare mauve drape to the side on its shower rod. You could almost call the collection of half-sized metal cubbyholes behind it a locker room. Cast offs from local high schools, their sizes and colors didn't match, like eggs from local farm chickens. Some were tan, some blue, some green, some half sized, a few accommodated long pants.

I sat on a makeshift bench of stacked milk crates in front of my personal strongbox of sweat. What hung from the hook inside wasn't a red card that told me I was cut from the ball team. But it was just as shocking to see it through the vents in my locker door that morning. I spun the combination wheel and opened it.

4

52-25

* * *

The metal door scraped open. Stuck on the central hook before me hung an unclaimed Lady Liberty Quick Draw card. Two numbers for the New York lottery were circled in red marker: 52 and 25. A pawn ticket from a shop on Water Street was stapled to its back.

I slid the cards into a coat pocket, then shoved the stuff from my locker into my gym bag, a blue and white premium gift from my surgery at Memorial Sloan Kettering Cancer Center. A moment later, I handed it to Happy. "Go ahead and check it. I'm out of here."

Happy dumped the bag's contents onto a table and inspected each item as thoroughly as if I was a tattooed terrorist. He said, "You know, your X is on that sign-in list this morning."

I said, "I'll need to use my one phone call to tell the president I can't leave town." Happy glared at me. "That's what I mean, Wolfe. Nobody likes it when you pull rank. Get out of here," he said. He turned and rejoined the grim squad.

I snapped a shot of Jack's register book with my phone before I creaked my way down the dark stairway with my bag in hand. The three names that signed in were familiar. When I reached the street I faced another decision.

Go after the pawn ticket or the suspects?

5

Ricky

* * *

I knew where he lived. He invited me over several times, all of which I declined. Not my type, if you know what I mean, and I think you do.

When I buzzed Ricky's third-floor walkup a couple blocks away, the door chime played the theme from *I Dream of Jeannie.* After the fisheye viewer behind the fuchsia door darkened, then lightened again, Ricky stood before me in his day wear with a hand on one hip. The Cuban exile's black silk pajamas featured white piping, with a pink pocket square. His broad smile of Chiclet teeth beneath a black pencil-thin mustache resembled two rows of piano ivories.

"Nicky!" he exclaimed. "What a fabulous surprise!"

I didn't have time for chit-chat. I said, "Jack's dead." The poor guy looked like I slapped him in the face with a cold fish. "Sorry," I said. "Tell me about your time at the gym today."

Ricky's energy left his body. He felt the tops of chairbacks as if blind and found his way to a tufted white leather sofa. When he sat he looked exhausted. "Nicky–excuse me. You hit me hard. Give me a minute."

I waited. Finally, after sitting in deep silence, he said, "I don't know. Same as usual, I guess." He looked up at me through reddened eyes. "When? How?"

"This morning. We're not sure. Who did you see? Anyone or anything unusual? Anything you can remember?"

"Same old thing, Nicky. I get there at eight. So do Millidge and Mike. They were there. Jack opened up, we all went up, just the usual small talk. I did my thing; walked home."

I looked him over, then asked, "Anybody see you leave, or come home?"

He tried to feign a polite laugh. "Pigeons?"

"Nothing else? No happy talk with Jack? No office coffee posse?"

Ricky's body shuddered at the thought. "Never! That black tar of his? No way. And we all left together. Same as usual. They went their way, I went mine." I knew Millidge and Mike. Their way was over toward Chinatown.

Chez Ricky was decorated by a member of the American Society of Interior Designers: Ricky. His dining area in a corner of the apartment looked like the interior of *Jeannie's* bottle. I liked classical art and sculpture as much as anyone but drew the line at gilding the lily. Discobolus was a beautiful sculpture without the gold paint and red lipstick.

After a moment, he remembered he had a guest. "I have some coffee you might find more palatable, Nick. Organic, whole beans, grown at 4,400 feet in Peru."

I said, "Sorry. Look, Ricky. I need to move fast and sometimes that hits hard."

"What do the police say?" he asked.

"I'm sure you'll see them, too," I said. "I got here first."

As I closed the door to his place behind me, Ricky broke down into mournful sobs.

Lieutenant Ralph "Happy" Moynihan passed me on my way down as he climbed the stairs. "I told you to stay out of this," he said.

"Just visiting friends," I replied. I gave a quick two-fingered salute. "See you in St. Looey."

"Is that where you're headed?"

"Maybe. After I get my hands on the killer." I pushed through the door to the street and heard his voice as it carried down the stairs.

"Wolfe!"

6

Millidge

* * *

A hack drove me through foggy drizzle to Hester Gardens between the Lower East Side, Little Italy, and Chinatown. I didn't know which flat in the brick and glass architecture belonged to Millidge Taylor, but I knew I'd find it. There were only 61 units.

The concierge doorman buzzed upstairs, listened, held the entry open for me. Two doors down from the elevator on the third floor, his brother Mike peeked at me through the slim opening allowed by their brass chains. His puzzled look fit his questions. "Hello, Wolfe. Just in the neighborhood?"

I said, "I need to talk to you guys about this morning."

The door closed. I heard a muffled quick conversation. After the metal-on-metal sounds of one sliding door chain followed by another, the door opened. I saw Millidge Taylor twenty feet in front of me. He faced me as he stood before a window with a view of Hester Street behind him.

His salt and pepper hair looked like it was coiffed that day, and every day. Perfect hair, perfect smile, perfect tan, perfect suit, perfect tie. I was suspicious of perfect people; they never were. His not-so-perfect brother Mike held the door open for me.

I only knew them from occasional encounters at the gym. Mike was muscular, practiced his Tae Kwon Do in Jack's boxing ring. I saw him spar a couple of times. His training was good, but he wasn't smooth. He was too self-absorbed, showed off his form, which made him as predictable as a clock. They way he telegraphed his moves, my nickname for him became Morse, Mike Morse.

Millidge began. "So, the infamous Mr. Wolfe. To what do we owe the honor of this visit to our humble abode?"

"It's Jack," I said.

Mike walked up and interjected. "We just saw him this morning. Is he OK? Does he need us to come back or something?"

"No," I said. They sensed the gravity in my voice. The brothers stood silent, waited. I said, "Somebody murdered him a couple hours ago."

The eyes of the Taylor brothers froze in shock. Their mouths gaped and followed suit. Millidge found his way to sit in a zebra hide chair. Mike plopped down on a red leather sofa. He asked, "What happened?"

"I got there at 10:30. He was killed an hour before. Ricky says you guys all left at nine?"

"That's right," said Millidge. The guy had a quick and fast mind. His statement was swift, clear and calm. They were a sibling team of property flippers. Millidge had brains; Mike did their legwork. The leg man spoke. "We have a daily Uber Black driver. He'll document our drive home and the time."

"That's interesting, Mike. I didn't ask about you guys. Ricky's the one who told me you left the same time he did."

The brothers exchanged furtive looks. I kept my hands inside my coat pockets, said, "Why so concerned about your alibi? I didn't ask for one."

"Just saying," said Mike. "You're some kind of shamus or something. You come in here and tell us Jack's been killed. Why else would you be here if you're not trying to frame us or something?"

I asked, "Did you see anything unusual? Anyone stand out to you? Outside on the street, maybe?"

"What is this!" said Mike. He stood up from the sofa. "The police should be the ones asking these questions. Who the Hell do you think you are, coming in here and interrogating us like this?"

Millidge was calm. He said from his chair, "Mike, don't make things worse than they are."

His brother stood up directly in front of me, a wild look in his eyes. I said, "You'll get your chance with the cops." I looked straight at Mike. "And just like you, Jack's killer will wish they got to him, first."

Mike Morse lived up to his nickname. I read his mind through his eyes. The telegraph message that foretold his next move beeped at me in a set of dots and dashes: "Tornado Kick." Mike was left-handed and stood with his body perpendicular to mine. He stepped forward and turned his hips. As usual, he tried to impress us with his moves. I've watched Dutch windmills turn faster than his spin that lifted his left leg into the launch position. Then his right leg unleashed his 540-degree flying kick.

But the Morse code I read in his eyes prepared me. The instant his right leg whipped through I blocked it with my left forearm. He was stuck, static for an instant with his left foot on the ground and his right foot up in the air.

My fist flew out of my pocket and came to the party wearing a coat of brass knuckles. I smashed a right cross straight into the soft tissue of his testicles with brick-breaking force. He collapsed and writhed on the floor in extreme anguish.

I stood, watched, looked over at his brother. Millidge kept his seat, his hands still folded on his lap. He spoke to his brother as Mike thrashed about and clutched his *cojones*. "That was unnecessary, Mike," he said. "Now, see what you've done?"

Millidge looked up at me. "I can assure you, Mister Wolfe, we were completely unaware of this tragic news until you arrived. I'm afraid we don't have anything that will help you. We got there as usual. Opened up with Jack, as usual. Worked out and departed, as usual. And we've been enjoying our breakfast here at our table since." He looked again at his brother. "Until you joined us."

I looked at Mike, twisting in his throes of anguish at my feet. Millidge said, "I can see this troubles you deeply. I'm sorry."

I got what I wanted. There was nothing else there. "Yeah," I said. "So am I." I leaned over Mike. His face was purple and the cords stuck out on both sides of his neck. He gnashed his teeth and groaned. Both of his hands clutched his nuts as I grabbed him by his collar, dragged him across the floor to a wall.

I yanked him up by his shoulders then slammed him down on his ass, hard. I turned to his brother and said, "That'll relieve the cause of his distress. You got any pain killers?"

"We keep Vicodin and Demerol on hand. This isn't his first outburst."

I said, "Have him chase one of those with a shot of whiskey and pack some ice around it. He'll be good in a couple of hours."

I turned to leave. Mike's guttural agonies subsided into soft whines. His quick relief from the excruciating pain delivered by my delicate medical procedure showed in the relaxed expression on his face.

With his elbows on the arms of his chair, Millidge steepled his fingers, called to me as I left. "Doctor Wolfe." I stopped at the door. "Thank you for your prescription remedy. I liked Jack. I hope you find whoever it is you're looking for. But if this is how you conduct conversations with your acquaintances, I shudder to think what will happen when you find his killer."

I said, "So do I. Give my regards to Lieutenant Moynihan."

"Who is that?" he asked.

The knock on the door was almost too well timed. Almost.

7

Cops

* * *

The clouds parted while I was inside and bright sunlight glazed the pavement. I hiked toward the East River through my reflections in the remaining pavement puddles, too buried in thought to consider transportation.

At Bowery Street I stopped and waited with the crowd for a green light's permission to cross. The cigarette I found in my pocket was my last one. Bent. The flame from my lighter found the remains of its ragged end and I inhaled a deep drag. The smoke worked its way through the labyrinth of my intake pathway, then escaped to freedom through my nose.

I stood at the front of the multitude on the curb and waited for the crossing light while my mind's computer processed 20 possible solutions to 15 real problems. The pair of beat cops across the street nearly escaped my notice.

When the throng of humanity stepped onto the glistening, wet asphalt, my eyes picked up the men in blue. Then I noticed their eyes. I put one of mine on them as I crossed, sensed my flank with the other.

The afternoon pedestrian traffic surrounded me and I blended in as much as I could. The blue uniforms moved through the throng of people and pressed forward at me. Not toward me, at me. The cops' eyes bored holes through my head. Each one wore a stern, dedicated purpose on his face.

They moved through people, around people, came closer. I was familiar with the faces of MPs intent on apprehension from my fun times in the service. The uniformed beat cops wore the same expressions. *What the Hell is this? What did I do? If these are Happy's guys, I'm going to ...*

One of them came at me on my right shoulder, the other approached on my left. I stopped, rooted myself into an anticipatory stance. When they brushed past, my surprise was surpassed only by my relief. I turned among the tight mob of street crossers and looked back. The guy they grabbed was only a foot behind me: late twenties, scruffy and unkempt in a pair of jeans and a white T-shirt. A faded gray sweatshirt was tied around his waist.

One of the cops grabbed his hands and yanked them both behind his back. The other cop reached his hand down and behind the knot that was tied in the guy's sweatshirt sleeves at his belt buckle. The smatchet he slid out glinted in the cloud-filtered sunlight.

I hadn't seen one in years, watched as the blade's extensive length grew. It came out further, slid further, then further, until the officer's hand was up to his shoulder. By the time he liberated it from the thug's pants, the glittering steel was almost as long as his torso. The smatchet was developed in WWII as a pure combat weapon, a combination between a machete and a bolo. Sixteen-and-a-half inches of double-sharpened and double-deadly steel.

I stood and stared. The two officers didn't pay attention to me; the punk was the principle subject on their minds. I approached, kept a safe distance. "Thanks, officers. What gives?"

One of them said, "Don't worry about it, buddy. We've got this."

I said, "You guys know about the murder at Jack's Gym?" The other cop nodded. I said, "Jack was stabbed in the back, probably with an icepick." I looked at the kid. He saw the destruction that came at him through my eyes.

I flashed my P.I. license in my wallet. "Nick Wolfe," I said. "I'm a private investigator. I'm sure Lieutenant Moynihan at homicide will want to talk to him." I closed in, stood toe to toe in front of the thug, added, "Or you can leave him alone with me for a few minutes of counseling."

One of the cops said, "Nick Wolfe? Aren't you getting a medal today at the White House? I saw it in the paper this morning."

His partner said, "No kidding? This is *the* Nick Wolfe?" He turned to me, offered his handshake. "It's an honor, sir. My boy thinks you're the greatest."

The perp saw his chance and made a move to break free. My system contained a certain amount of pent-up angst I needed to relieve. I decked him with a right cross that would have punched a hole through a wall.

The cops looked at each other. *Maybe that wasn't such a good idea ...* "Have a good day, sir," said one of them. They lifted the thug's limp body from the asphalt and dragged him off.

"Wait," I said. "What's his name? I'd like some ID on the guy who just tried to shiv me in the back."

One of the officers said, "Sir, did he actually assault you in any way?"

"No," I admitted.

He said, "He matches the description of a bodega robbery. You can inquire for the report at the station."

His partner waved, said, "We'll take care of this, sir. Please, stay safe." They dragged him off. I continued on my way, oblivious to the bolt from the blue about to hit me.

8

Avalon

* * *

T he seven-block greenway ahead caught me by surprise. Sara D. Roosevelt Park was the last thing on my mind. The familiar inner-city site for fun and games lay directly in my path. Street food aromas from a nearby stand beckoned. A hot dog and cup of coffee later, a vacant bench by the soccer field near Canal Street offered me a seat. I took a load off my feet and contemplated my situation amid the events of the morning.

God sent a flood to wash abominations off the face of the earth.
He sent Samson to destroy the Philistines.
And he sent me to sweep the scum off the streets.

But a paraphrase of the 1924 song "Big Bad Bill is Sweet William Now" by Milton Ager and Jack Yellen started playing in the back of my mind. It's a funny ragtime song about a big strong tough guy who gets married and settles down.

To begin, Electra and I recently celebrated our one-month anniversary and my newlywed wife wanted me to retire young (i.e. alive). At the least, she wanted me to move my investigative business into her White Mansion across the street from the White House.

I don't want to move to the armpit of bureaucracy; I love New York.

Also, I was supposed to be in the nation's capital. In twenty-four hours, I had an important appointment with POTUS.

I'm a covert guy from the Unit; I hate the hoopla and media attention. If I was out to sell books it would be great. But I'm not. It's bad for business.

On top of all that, my little sister, Trouble, was moving out of our East River warehouse. She met and fell for action movie star Josh Hitt at our wedding and during our south Texas firefight. His home in the Hollywood Hills awaited her and her Shih Tzu, Winston, as new Cali residents.

I'll miss our little big apple family; my warehouse is going to be quiet.

Regardless, one of my best friends was dead. *And I'm going to deliver the Code of Hammurabi lex talionis to Jack's killer, with maximum prejudice.*

On an engraved brass plaque, my park bench memorialized someone who must have been famous. I never heard of them. Dark clouds that moved in blanketed the field with a temporary darkness.

A green mesh circular file cabinet beside me identified itself as "Property of City Sanitation." It held a crumpled *New York*

Daily Mirror that announced with a two-inch headline, "PRESIDENTIAL MEDAL FOR NICK WOLFE." I pulled it out, whisked off some coffee grounds with the back of my hand and read about myself.

"Local private investigator, aka: the Pied Piper of Washington and Alamo hero, Nick Wolfe will receive the Presidential Medal of Freedom with Distinction from President John Jackson tomorrow afternoon in the White House Rose Garden."

Six weeks before, I stepped out of my Big Apple element and into south Texas. Electra and I exited our honeymoon train and got caught up in the biggest American firefight of the century. A motley force of volunteers and I saved Texas and America from 40,000 multi-national invaders at the Alamo Village in Brackettville It was a giant mess.

Inside the Alamo Village, as we awaited the final siege on Memorial Day morning, all I wanted was to sit on a Central Park bench with a Nathan's hot dog and a cup of coffee. *Here I am. Why don't I feel better?*

I let the *wienerwurst* warm my hand through its crinkled paper wrapper. Steam floated up and curled above the rim of the paper cup beside me on the bench. I removed my thin flask from my pocket and added a shot of bourbon to its flavor. It wasn't Central Park, and it wasn't a Nathan's Famous Coney Island Dog, but I was home. I was back in the city that never sleeps.

Below the puff piece about me on the front page I read the same collection of good news that was on my phone earlier: alcohol, drugs, murder, rape, terrorism, theft, war. Farmers weren't going to farm anymore, because bankers weren't going to bank anymore, because stockbrokers were broke, and the whole world was going to Hell in a handbasket. And so was I, because I was filling my brain with that garbage.

The USA was 250 years old, big birthday party plans were in motion nationwide, fentanyl still killed our people, the weapons truck on its way to Ukraine vanished, 300,000 children that crossed the southern border were still missing, and so was gold from Fort Knox.

A group of kids played with a soccer ball on the vacant field in front of me. *Please don't kick it to me. Please don't kick it to me.* The last time I stopped a ball in the rain I played catch with a nine-year-old kid coincidentally named Nick–and my entire life changed.

The boy was kidnapped later that night to be sacrificed by pedophiles beneath the nation's capital. *Washington Post* headlines hung the "Pied Piper of Washington" moniker on me when I rescued him and a couple dozen other high profile kids from their netherworld chambers. I say "high profile" because his mom was, at the time, Mrs. Electra White, the wealthiest widow in the world.

And I say "at the time" because six months later we were married in the Rose Garden when she became Mrs. Electra Wolfe. During our honeymoon at her south Texas ranch headquarters, we got caught up in our little border skirmish.

A thousand volunteers comprised of the Texas Army 3rd Brigade, TEXIAN motorcycle club and 1836 period reenactors defended an invasion of our southern border at the Alamo Village in Brackettville, Texas. I should probably mention three counties of stampeding cattle as well.

I thought things would normalize when I returned to New York, stepped down off the train, bit into a Famous Nathan's in Central Park. I was wrong. The president wanted me back in the Rose Garden, in D.C. My wife wanted me home, in D.C.

Don't kick it to me. Please, don't kick it to me. They kicked it to me. The ball bounced in my direction, its bounding arcs diminishing in height as it approached. I sat and waited to catch it with reluctant, open hands.

A passing jogger swept in front of me for an interception. The ball soared back out to midfield from their quick running kick. The passerby looked back toward me, waved.

Nonplussed, I blindly returned the gesture. The only thing I noticed about the person was a smile. Big, bright, perfect white teeth flashed beneath the shade of the clouds overhead. *Some cosmetic dentist's kids went to college on those ivories.*

The nondescript runner in baggy sweats turned back in my direction. I didn't know who it was, but she seemed familiar when her European accent asked, "Nick?" with two ee's in *Nick.* Then, those eyes. She slipped out of her shades and from within the shadow of a navy hoodie two glinting luminosities of cobalt blue pierced the gray air like searchlights. There was only one pair of eyes on earth like hers.

When she threw back her hood and tossed her hair, she was unfamiliar no longer. I would have recognized her across Grand Central Station. The face of the world's top model graced a thousand magazine covers.

She was so ... Continental. Her vivid blue eyes smiled at me from within the infallible facial bone structure of elven royalty. Platinum blonde locks in a princess bob haircut framed her visage. She laughed and offered her hand. *"Je suis désolée,"* she said. She indicated her deliberately nondescript attire. "I am sorry. I travel incognito."

Maybe I was dumbstruck; maybe I was star struck; maybe I had so much going on in my mind I didn't have room for comment. I looked at her, speechless.

The gorgeous French model made her people all but forget about their illustrious national treasure, Brigitte Bardot. With that seductive French accent, her voice was at once soft and appealing. She was surprised that I seemed taken aback and said, *"Je suis,* Avalon. I see you at Jack's Gym."

As if she needs the addition of a woman's sexy French accent to add to her allure. She? Has seen—me? Electra didn't marry me for my looks. This was the first uplifting encounter I'd had all day. We shook hands and I feigned a smile. "Of course," I said.

We had never spoken; Jack's wasn't a meat market for monthly members. The unwritten decorum meant we generally left each other alone for serious training in strength and combat sports. That didn't mean I didn't notice her. That didn't mean that during her workouts everyone in the gym didn't do everything they could not to stare. I understood why she went out in baggy clothes and dark glasses.

I also understood her need for self-defense work in the ring. She drew men like a neodymium magnet, and they weren't all royalty, if you know what I mean, and I think you do. She imported her own *Silat* instructor for weekly practice in Jack's square circle.

At the gym, Avalon didn't dress to be seen. As now, she dressed to be unseen in non-branded training gear; no makeup, no jewelry, nothing provocative. She didn't need it. If she stood barefoot in a burlap sack her natural attributes would be as breathtaking as the sunrise on Maui at the top of Mount Haleakala.

Her face reacted to mine. The Cupid's bow of her lips parted and she spoke softly, "You look unhappy. I am sorry."

"Thanks," I said. "I've got a lot on my mind."

She tried to get me to smile. "You should join me. *Maintenant,* I jog to Jack's. A workout together might clear your head?" She began to sing in a childlike voice: "*Et la tete, et la tete, alouette, alouette, Ohhhhhhh!*"

I looked up at her, drew in a deep breath, grimaced, let it out through my nose. I said, "Have a seat."

9

JUJU

* * *

I gave it to her in 25 words or less. My teeth were clenched to keep me from saying anything else. I faced front.

Avalon.

Her unique face was at the stage where a blush of youth persists in women's features as they mature into their true beauty. Her cover girl days would fade someday, but it would be years before she modeled *prêt-à-porter*. During the previous decade, she was the top draw for couture runways, perfume commercials, and hundreds of magazine covers. The top fashion model cost over a million bucks a shoot.

Hers was the pinup behind Jack's desk we admired most. Miscolored push pins affixed a glossy magazine fold-out page of her smooth beauty, juxtaposed against the rough, paint-peeled walls. Avalon's flawless Riviera-tanned complexion glowed through fine beads of workout precipitate that her handlers had meticulously applied. Her ash-blonde bob haircut surrounded those piercing eyes in her breathtaking, unforgettable face.

In the photo, her upturned breasts jutted skyward with firm peaks beneath a yellow top that clung to her skin like a wet sail in the wind. Nobody knew her away from the gym, but she was our own, our Jack's Gym Juju.

I sat with her in silence. The face recognized worldwide as exciting and alluring turned upside down behind a mask of tragedy. I put my arm around her. After a few moments she spoke. "*Quelle dommage.* I am sorry. You came here to be alone."

"I'm on my way home," I said. "I was chasing down clues."

We stayed that way together, alone and quiet on the park bench. After the third squirrel scampered away from us empty handed, Avalon straightened her sitting posture. "You were close to him?" she asked, with two ee's in *him*.

I reached into my pocket for a cigarette, tried the other pocket. *Where the Hell are my cigarettes?* I rustled through my pants pockets, finally found the crushed box in my back pocket. Out of nine lung darts, one wasn't mangled too much. *Where's my lighter! Damn it! If I lost my ...* I felt around in my pockets, found it, lit up, then said, "After ten years of military service, the VA sent me home with stage three colon cancer. The Big Casino. Nothing more they could do. After my workout one day, I found an index card taped inside my locker. All that was on it was a phone number."

"Jack's?" she asked.

My lungs coughed up an involuntary puff. "No," I said. "It was the direct line to the Chief of Surgery at Josie Robertson Surgery Center of Memorial Sloan Kettering. Up at 61st and York. Jack got me in to the number one colon oncology surgeon in the world.

"The U.S. government sent me home so my sister could accept my coffin flag while a bugler played Taps. Jack made a phone call. Cashed in a favor. I got fixed. I'm alive. Yeah, you could say we were close."

She said, "I feel anger inside you, besides your grief."

"I'm not going to get mad," I said. "I'm going to get even. And it's going to cost the killer, if you know what I mean, and I think you do."

She sat, silent, then abruptly shifted her posture into the attitude of a stiff upper lip. "Well, my afternoon is unexpectedly open. What are your plans, *Monsieur* Wolfe?"

My coffee concoction was cold. I reached into a pocket for the pawn and lottery tickets, examined them as she looked on. "I'm headed to Two Bridges. This was hanging in my locker when I cleaned it out this morning."

She said, "I have never been in a pop shop. May I tag with you?"

10

NOHO

* * *

When you've been around the block 5,000 times, and you know that you know without having to think that you know, because you just know, the odds are you're more correct than all the Cray supercomputers and experts on the subject, combined.

You don't need reams of data and committees of experts on the subject. Because you've been there. And you know that you've been there. They've only heard about it, read about it, studied it.

You lived it, and you know that you know. And you know you're right. Some call it "thin slicing." I call it "hip shooting." And I never miss.

"Yes," I said. "I mean, no, I don't want you to tag with me. I mean, tag along. I mean I don't want you to tag along. This is business. I work alone. Sorry."

She added a lilt to her voice in a polite attempt to lighten my mood. She squeezed my arm and said, "I promise, I won't say a thing, darling."

I always heard that cobalt blue was an impossible eye color in humans. I allowed myself to examine hers, just to find out, of course. What I saw hit me hard. My mind's eye instantly conjured a suppressed vision: *Don't ever do that again! Victoria Taylor had enchanting tourmaline green eyes beneath jet black hair; murdered in her D.C. art gallery because she helped me. She was gorgeous, strong, independent–and dead.*

"No," I said. "Your life belongs on runways, inside photo studios, at penthouse cocktail parties. I live at street-level in pawn shops, diners and bars."

Through a polite smile and with quiet sarcasm she added, "And worn-out, old-school gyms?"

"Come on," I said. "I'll see you home."

She smiled. "*Merci.* That would be nice."

"I hope it isn't the Upper West Side," I said. "I'm at the end of Montgomery Street on the East River."

"I thought you knew, darling. I live in NOHO, just a few blocks away."

Avalon lived in La La Land. NOHO (North Of HOuston Street) is the perfect central Manhattan location for an international high fashion model. The triangular slice of the city thrives between SOHO (South Of HOuston Street), University Village, East Village, and the Lower East Side.

A newsstand along the way featured the current issue of *Women's Wear Daily* on its sidewalk rack. I couldn't help picking up a copy. I examined the stunning face on its cover, lowered the *holiday* fashion week edition and looked at the same pair of eyes in 3D. As I returned my gaze to the two-dimensional print version of the real thing that stood beside me, I sarcastically said, "You poor little girl."

She protested. "You have no idea," she said. "My entire childhood I was *le vilain petit canard*." Her face had changed; it wasn't happy.

My French was not good. I had learned Swahili a lot faster. "What's that?" I asked.

"*Le vilain petit canard* is the ugly duckling in the fairy tale." She looked down, shook her head. Her voice was soft. "People, they were very mean."

"Really? You?" My introspection took an introspective look at itself: *What an in-depth, intelligent question.* My thoughts were on a dozen other things, and it showed. *I'm one-on-one with Avalon, and I can't even concentrate on her!*

She looped her arm through mine as we passed some street-level art galleries and bistros. I observed the reflection of the model's face in the glass of a big window when she paused. Inside, an easel featured an oil painting of an impressionistic seaside scene. After a moment's viewing, she said, "*Plage des*

Catalans. Marseille. My home." She sighed and closed her eyes. "Golden sand."

I heard what she said but was still wrestling inside myself. *Nice painting.* I said, "What?"

"Marseille," she said. "My home."

At the "graffiti gate" for 40 Bond Street, a collection of near-Italianate condos, she paused. "*Arrêtez-vous ici.* This is where I get off," she said, then giggled. "So, to speak."

Before renovated storehouse lofts became *avant-garde*, NOHO was an industrial warehouse district. When the Beautiful People began snapping up their hip Bohemian properties, apartment prices in the fashion-forward area went ballistic. Each flat cost several million, a few blocks northeast from Jack's two-bit, second-story gym on Grand Street.

I said, "Quite a bit different from my waterfront warehouse digs in the Lower East Side."

"*Monsieur* Nick!" she said with a smile. "*Vous êtes un Bohémien!*"

"Just a big old empty warehouse space now. But this ..." I looked upward at her building's exterior of copper and mirror-polished stainless steel.

She said, "I have had thoughts of moving."

Moving was on my mind as well. I said, "You wouldn't be interested in a three-story warehouse on the East River, would you? Riverfront property, with a view?"

Avalon laughed. "I meant Monaco, darling. May I invite you in? (again, with two ee's in *in*.) You could use a drink? Some company?"

Yeah, right. Just the kind of complication I need to heap on top of everything else. No way am I going to get myself alone with a hot and trendy member of the female persuasion in her hot and trendy Manhattan high rise. And of all hot and trendy females to turn down, this one is Avalon.

MIT scientists used modern equipment in a clinical setting to determine how fast we comprehend images in our minds. They measured that we identify an image in exactly 13 microseconds, or .0013 seconds. At that rate, we take in and process 769 images per second. All day long.

The interesting thing is, other people see us and read *us* at the rate of 769 images per second. All day long. Professional poker players make or lose fortunes by reading or misreading the signals other people send out. And when you're sending out 46,140 images per minute–other people can read what you're thinking by what they're seeing. They can literally read your mind.

Within 1,538 images, Avalon read mine. "*Monsieur* Wolfe!" she said. She acted shamefully delighted; a charming laugh followed. "You feel uneasy. Do not worry. I have *un habitant* who can chaperone?" Her next laugh was more seductive. "You would like Senta, Nick. All the men like Senta."

11

Sol

* * *

I turned her over to Carlton, her doorman, and caught a hack to Two Bridges by the East River, half a mile south of my place. Behind his two-inch-thick Lexan window, Sol Steinberg studied my pawn ticket. His snap-on glasses looked like they were glued to his pronounced proboscis, beneath watery hazel eyes and a balding head of thin white hair.

He peered at me over his nose spectacles. "This is Jack's ticket," he said. "Why is it that you have it, young sir who is not Jack?"

I told him. He hung his head, let out a deep breath. Sol took the ticket, stepped to one side. It took the old guy a minute to look up a phone number in an ancient Rolodex card file. He dialed his black rotary hard line phone, spoke in a low tone, listened.

After he hung up the receiver, he returned and laid the ticket on his counter. "So, you're *that* Nicholas Wolfe?" he asked. "This is so sad. So tragic." He looked directly into my eyes. "He's a good man, you know. Jack is a good man."

Sol laid a hand on top of the ticket. "I know this item," he said. "I had a feeling. Such a feeling I had. It isn't normal, you know."

"What do you mean?" I asked. "What isn't normal?" I thought, *for that matter, what in my life is normal?*

He shuffled off. "One minute," he said.

I looked around at the random items on display for sale: tools, jewels, watches, the *de rigeur* hocked guitars and drum sets. A moment later, Sol returned. Whatever he deposited on the floor behind his counter settled with a resounding slam. "Ninety smackers," he said.

"How long have you had it here?" I asked.

He took a step back. "So now, no wonder! You're a friend of Jack's. So now you haggle about the money? Yes, not even a week!" He examined the ticket. "Four days."

"No. I'm wondering how long ago Jack left it so I can figure out what was going on at the time. I'm asking you to help me catch Jack's killer."

"You couldn't have said so? You're killing *me*, here! Like I said, just this week; four days ago. I have written it right here. Yes, the 25th. Thursday."

I handed him a C note. He cleaned and jerked Jack's pawn item up onto the countertop. With a gentle backhand wave of both hands he said, "Good. Now it's yours. Take it. I'm happy to have it gone."

I lifted the distinguished leather briefcase to leave. It yanked my hand down to the floor, heavy as Hell. "Why so relieved?" I asked. "What's in here?"

He looked down his nose over his lowered glasses, up at me. "That's what I said. It isn't the kind of thing normal people pawn. You know, normal people: crooks, junkies, addicts, musicians. What's a briefcase? A box with something in it."

He shrugged and continued. "What is in it? I do not know. I do know one thing. My friend Jack is dead and some shamus I hear about in the news shows up the same day with Jack's claim check."

He leaned forward and looked out his front window, both directions. I said, "Sol, it could be his bug-out bag."

In Sol's face I saw my second-grade teacher, Mrs. Schumacher. Her expression through her glasses registered her disappointment at my vain attempt to alibi myself out of another scrape. To be sure, it was Sol who stood before me, but the glasses lowered on his nose and the face behind them belonged to Mrs. Schumacher.

The elegant attaché case's appearance was deceiving. It was thin, covered in smooth cordovan leather, with a cylinder lock on each gold-plated clasp. For such a fine, smooth leather exterior, it carried the weight of a packed toolbox inside.

I said, "If you think of anything about Jack or your deal on whatever this thing is, give me a call." He inspected my engraved .45 ACP calling card as he rolled it in his fingertips.

"I hope you catch this killer person, Nicholas. Jack deserves it."

12

Murgatroyd

* * *

I flagged down another cab to my office to finish the day. A few minutes later, I stepped off the stomach-dropping 21-floor express elevator ride to my Lower East Side office suite.

When I pushed through our double glass doors, Donna looked up with a funny smile that played across her lips. The official title of my attractive office manager was Gal Friday.

She and our officially titled IT Junkie Flunky, Norm, were hired soon after I made Murgatroyd a partner in the firm. My four-person private investigative company had been a one-person operation until that day.

* * *

One morning five years ago, my printer didn't. It refused to execute a big new contract and I grumbled about squandering time and energy on menial office tasks.

Meanwhile, James Murgatroyd Fontenot got off the elevator on the wrong floor to interview with a video game development company downstairs and blindly ambled into our office. I seized on the opportunity of his technical skill sets and while I conquered the complicated task of making coffee, Murgatroyd fixed the machine. I persuaded him to come aboard for real combat games, instead of the virtual kind.

A high-tech junkie, he kept his finger on the pulse of the tech world by the hour. And he displayed an uncanny sixth sense to prepare for my immediate future needs. Yet he dressed as though he lived and worked in a 1940s Midwest bank. I wanted very much to call him Jeeves, settled for his middle name, Murgatroyd.

Under his stewardship, our offices became a juxtaposition of high technology and antique furniture. A wall of glaring laser TVs were powered by the newest, fastest computers. We ran a 5G internet connection with over a gig of download speed. And Art Deco furnishings were complemented with British Bombay tables and classic Baccarat crystal.

When I interviewed applicants for Gal Friday, Donna Mona Lisa stood out in open-toed stiletto heels with tight black jeans and a silver silk blouse that set off her shoulder-length raven hair. While several applicants sat and waited, Donna saw the confusion when the phones rang, monitored the traffic between my interviews and Murgatroyd's, and aided the entry of a local news team for an interview. She got up, pitched in and took over the office functions. She listed the names of the applicants, answered the phones, kept me posted on exactly what was happening and who was next to interview. By the time I got to her, my sole interview question was, "Can you type?" I hired her on the spot.

I thought, *Donna is a Brooklyn girl. Will she move to D.C.? Will Norm? Murgatroyd?*

She placed her late afternoon call to her mother on hold. In a playful, sarcastic voice she said, "Good morning, Boss."

I said, "Hello, gorgeous. Got anything for me?"

"In your office," she said.

I let a cigarette dangle from my lower lip. In a bad imitation of a film-noir detective I said, "A rich redhead whose husband's having an affair?"

"Yes," she said.

"You're joking."

Donna's voice was easy on the ears. She spoke through a wry smile, "She's brunette, bossy and has a very large bodyguard."

I asked, "Really? How large would that be?"

"Large enough," she said with an impish grin. I had to admit, my Italian Gal Friday had good taste in men. Her boyfriend Louis worked on Wall Street: handsome, professional, well-educated and well mannered. "She's waiting in your office," she said.

I whispered, "I haven't arrived yet. I need to see Murgatroyd."

"He's in his office."

When I opened my business partner's door, I inhaled the scent of CK One. The room was lit by incandescent bulbs from living room floor lamps, coffee table lamps and the green banker's desk lamp on his right side.

The moment I entered, he looked up from his papers, said, "I know about Jack."

Little about Murgatroyd surprised me. The New Orleans native exhibited intuition that was quicker and deeper than the thinking of most sophisticated logicians. And he was very often right. I called it his Voodoo Logic. I said, "What do you know?"

"Don't be surprised," he said. "Police scanner. Suspected murder."

"And?"

"And, I know you. I know we might as well put everything else on hold. I know that whatever plans you had this morning are different now. I know Trouble is on her way to L.A. and I know you're supposed to be with the President of the United States in ..." Murgatroyd's daily attire came from an armoire full of suits, every one of them three-pieces. He pulled his gold pocket watch from his vest. "Less than 24 hours."

"Very good," I said. "Do you know we may be moving our operations to Washington, D.C.?"

"Not until now," he said. "But it was only a matter of time. I mean, is Electra McDonald-White-Wolfe going to move out of the White Mansion—a two-acre, five-story, 60,000 square foot estate across 15th Street from the White House—to live in the Bowery?"

I smiled. "Lower East Side," I corrected. "And, it *is* riverfront property."

We shared mutual bemusement at the contrast. I asked, "So, what do you think?"

"I think I need a drink," he said. "You?"

"Double bourbon," I said. "Long day." After a moment I amended my order. "I needed a double at 10:30 this morning. Make it a triple."

He poured two glasses of amber liquid from a collection of decanters near his desk. Jim Beam for me, Southern Comfort for him. Mine was taller. My business partner said, "I'd have to make some adjustments, find a place to live."

I said, "Hell, we'll have the entire fifth floor penthouse. 12,000 square feet. We'll build it out to suit. When you live at the White Mansion you have servants, chefs, central D.C. location, and no rent payments."

It took him two seconds. "You drive a hard bargain," he said with a grin. "I'm in."

I asked, "What about Donna and Norm? They're loyal New Yorkers."

"We've talked about it," he said. "They're rooted here. Until your honeymoon party train trip to Texas, Donna never left the city."

"Well, if they can't make it, I understand. I want to take care of them. We could give them a two years' severance package."

The man who managed our books didn't contain his surprise at my generosity. "I don't think they'd complain about that!" he said. "But I'll meet with them. Who knows, they might want to move there, too. Would they get the same lodging benefit?"

The math that answered his question was easy. "12,000 square feet. 6,000 for the office. 2,000 for each person's private living apartment times three people." I said, "Look, I haven't decided anything yet, so just inquire. I want to talk with them myself. Right now, I've got to meet somebody in my office."

The man with family on Avery Island, Louisiana said, "You'll tag her *Tabasco.*"

13

Cocks

* * *

I saw her from behind as she examined the artifacts and case mementos on my walls. Her red slim-waisted one-piece suit nodded back to the eighties, with subtler shoulder pads and a wide black belt. I knew her the moment she turned.

Some women look hotter in business than they do at dinner or in a bar. She was one of them. She was a member of the Manhattan hot, wealthy, single, sex kitten set. My supposition was Upper East Side.

I'm not talking about career women who are attractive, or look nice, or exhibit a subtle air of sophistication. I'm talking about animalistic heat, cat on a hot tin roof heat, smoldering, take me now or forever hold your regret, heat.

She was tall at 5'8" and stood 6' 0" in heels where her pretty, fine features allowed her eyes to take center stage. They were beautiful deep blue eyes, outdone only by her long, well-shaped, tan legs. She wore her hair in a layered cut that gave the media mogul the look of a latent wild fling ready to go down. I remembered how she looked in her track suit, naked underneath, with bouncing motions beneath its fabric that weren't caused by her gams.

The year before at the annual Birknerhaus Group meeting she whispered to me, "I own 55 radio stations and the top-rated television network." That was at their orgy in the hotel's massive subterranean chambers before I burned the place down.

"Natalie Cocks," I said. I nodded toward her elephantine companion. "Who's your bum of the month?"

The brunette's dark hair swirled as she spun around. When she saw me she lifted a pair of black Ray Bans above her eyes with a thumb and forefinger. "Nick!" She gave a cursory glance across the room to her gargantuan bodyguard.

The guy appeared as if his tailor ran out of fabric. His top-stitched sharkskin suit was expensive, if due only to the vast yardage of fabric required to cover his mass. I figured him for a professional wrestler turned bodyguard; subconsciously nicknamed him, Carl Colossal.

I stood 6' 4" and Carl's massive bulk made me look like a middleweight. He was handsome enough, maybe he was her boyfriend. I hoped I didn't have to hurt him. It was the end of a long day and I wasn't in the mood. "Nicky," she said, "this is Cyrano Mangione. He accompanies me in town. Cyrano played right tackle for the Jets." Carl nodded with a stupid smile.

Her shades were parked on her forehead above her sable eyebrows. Their small white dot on one corner gave her away. I asked, "Do you have enough storage in your spyglass camera for everything? Donna can provide you with a thumb drive about our firm."

"Why, Nick," she declared, "what would make you think such a thing?"

I snatched her glasses, called for Donna. Carl bolted upright from his seat. Before he gained his footing I gave him a fast powerful shove back down into his chair.

"Time out," I said to him. "You're on the sidelines."

Donna walked in, or I should say, well, I don't know how to say it; she moved, she sashayed, she strutted. None of those single words work, but when she walked, Donna walked, and I watched poetry in motion to the strains of "Satin Doll." I stuck the shades into her open palm and said, "Drop these from the Empire State Building, will you?"

She raised a mirthful eyebrow. The corners of her upper lip made a playful wordless curl. She twirled the sunglasses by one ear stem, turned and walked out. Yes, Natalie Cocks was drop dead gorgeous, but Donna walked, in a way that attracted the eyes of male animals in any kingdom, phylum, class or species.

The lady that stood before me wasn't happy, but the matriarch of her self-acclaimed, "top-rated television network" maintained her composure. She said, "Really, Nick. I understand the cloak-and-dagger secrecy in your boorish business, but that doesn't give you the right to seize my personal property."

I asked, "How can I help you, Natalie?"

"I've seen you work," she said. "You're effective. Coarse, crude, but effective."

"I guarantee results," I said. "And I'm not cheap."

"Neither is my problem," she said.

"And what's that?" I glanced toward Carl Colossal.

"You can say anything in front of Cyrano," she said. "He goes everywhere with me." She turned to me with a roguish smirk. "As you like to say, 'If you know what I mean, and I think you do.'"

I didn't restrain my grin. My new desk chair's deep brown leather was embossed with the golden Seal of the Great State of Texas. Governor Stinson commissioned it as a token of appreciation for defending Alamo II on Memorial Day and I planned to thank him in person the next afternoon in the Rose Garden. I took a seat, found a cigarette and lit it with a flip of my Zippo. I motioned for her to take a seat next to Carl. "I don't have all day," I said.

"I know," she said. "I was surprised you were still in New York. You don't want to keep the leader of the free world waiting."

"What's up?" I asked.

"I'm being robbed," she said.

"Come again?"

The look she gave me seemed honest enough. "My programming. Our programming–The Cocks Network–it's being streamed all over Europe and the Middle East!"

"And that's illegal?" I asked.

"If it's done by a eurotrash company that's selling my network's original content and not paying me for it, it is! If the company claims to be a not-for-profit while they accept exorbitant financial backing from The Phone Company, it is!" (TPC was the ticker symbol for the world's largest privatized telephone network.)

"Sounds big. Where do I come in?"

"The problem is finding the money. It's billions of dollars. They launder it through the central banks of European nations. I know it. They know I know it. Everybody knows it. But I have to prove it.

"I need proof, Nick. Evidence. It requires a trip to Switzerland. We have to take on the Bank of Global Settlements." She pulled out a pack of Virginia Slims, set fire to one with a slender, gold Cartier lighter.

She spoke with a tinge of irritation. "You see what you did to me on St. Thomas? I didn't smoke. Now, I'm hooked on the damned things." She turned to one side and blew out a puff upward, toward the ceiling. "You need to leave with me as soon as possible after your ceremonies tomorrow."

I pushed back from my desk. "Sorry. I'm occupied," I said.

"But, Nick! This is important!"

"Not as important as what I'm working on."

"Whatever they're paying you, I'll triple it."

"Sorry," I said. "You need a civil guy. And I tend to be anything but."

Her face was frozen in a state of shock. "Nick!" she cried. "This is my entire empire! They're stealing everything we do!"

I liked Natalie. We had fun on St. Thomas Island before I sent her back to her room. I said, "I'm not discounting you or your problem. I have something I have to do. And I'm going to get it done, come Hell or high water, maybe both."

I had never seen her face turn sad. Shocked, disappointed, surprised, confused, but not sad. I said, "OK. Look, I can stay on top of it for you, but I'm committed to my case. I can only operate in a supervisory capacity."

"Meaning what?" she asked. She was almost in tears.

"I'm going to nail a murderer. I'm not taking my eye off those crosshairs for one second. I have a colleague who can handle this. He's great at civil investigations. I can oversee things for you."

"Nick, I know you. Who is this other person? Do I know him? How do I know if he's any good? I need results, big, important results. And I need them fast. We're hemorrhaging money because of this."

14

Roscoe

* * *

Roscoe Ritter operated from the second floor of our building. A few minutes after Donna called him, the corpulent detective strolled into our office. I tagged him, Mister Five by Five, five feet tall and five feet around. He benefitted from the fortunate circumstance that our office entry provided a pair of glass French doors. His double-wide body needed double-wide clearance.

He seemed never to be apart from his comical sidekick, any form of food. That day's companion was a Reuben sandwich from our building's streetside deli. The stack of sauerkraut inside its onion encrusted bun served in his vanguard as a stinking aromatic Herald that announced his pending arrival.

Roscoe's elevator ride afforded him time to conclude sliding into his glad rags. As he entered, he tucked a black shirt inside the pants of his butterscotch pinstripe suit with his available hand. A green bolo tie in the shape of a four-leaf clover stretched tightly around his neck as the fabric of his suit strained its buttons.

The round mound of sound flashed a broad smile that overwhelmed most people. His teeth were too many, too big, too something. He told me the first time he went to a dentist for a routine exam they x-rayed his mouth. He waited alone in the chair for an hour. When the doctor returned, he brought six other guys with him. Baffled by the x-rays, he went up and down the hall and recruited other doctors and dentists to witness his discovery.

That was when Mister Five by Five got used to people looking at him funny. Roscoe said nobody spoke. The ring of faces peered down at him as if he was a circus freak. He had eight wisdom teeth.

As Donna escorted him into our meeting through my office door, Roscoe ran a hand through his disheveled mop. It didn't make him camera ready. He took a bite from his Reuben. "So," he said. "I understand the boys in Switzerland are calling."

Natalie turned to me. Quicker than a Fox News host hocking their new book, she said, "No! No, no, no! Are you kidding me?" She took two steps back, observed him head to toe with appall. She looked at me again. "Absolutely not! We're dealing with huge sums of money! No!"

Roscoe was smart, innovative, and he didn't wear a gun. He didn't need to. Our clientele was different; his address book was respectable. We both got results, we just had different types of cases and employed different processes. His were civil; mine weren't.

I occasionally kibitzed cases of his when he needed a hammer for backup. His technique baffled me. It seemed he talked with someone about every unrelated subject under the sun: where they grew up, went to school, if they had kids, how they got their job. Then, out of left field and before I knew it, they opened up and bean-spilled their whole warehouse to him.

I greeted him across the desk with a handshake and introduced everyone. Roscoe nodded at Natalie, ignored Carl, took a seat on my desk. As I summarized the case, he lifted the lid of my humidor. One of my Cubans met his sniff-test approval. He appropriated it to his lapel pocket.

Roscoe was bright, he was intuitive, and his math teacher would have flunked him. He solved the problems but couldn't show his work. His insight cracked cases with non-sequitur metaphysics that wizards and brainiacs couldn't fathom.

On one case, I was with him when he made an impromptu side trip to the zoo. He waddled to a picnic table by the magpie exhibit, ate some peanuts, and had an epiphany.

His client was a Wall Street firm. The board room full of Ivy League executives were perplexed about $12,000,000 embezzled out their back door. Two different high-tech detective agencies charged them small fortunes. Both came up dry. Roscoe uncovered that the janitor, with a degree from DeVry, hacked their computers at night.

I asked him how he figured it out. His reply was as simple and direct as his solution. "Occam's razor," was all he said. Sadly, the same didn't hold true for his bets on the ponies. It seemed every time he made a major score on a case, a few days later he needed to find work again. My conjecture was, if you handicapped Roscoe's inherent intuitive genius with Murgatroyd's New Orleans Voodoo logic, added the statistics from trackside racing forms and threw in mystical Mexican mothers who bet horses because they liked their names, he still couldn't pick a winner.

He said, "So, I take it you're hoping this Bank of Global Settlements court finds in your favor for a hefty fine."

Natalie said, "A financial penalty, yes. But I want the revenue stream from my program content over there. The Bank of Global Settlements is headquartered in Schutzenmattpark. It's the central bank over all sovereign central banks. They're the ones that allow the financial trafficking of this extortion scam across national borders. I don't know that you would call it a court."

She turned to me, her eyes dewy and pleading for help. "Nick, I've been to three investigative agencies. Each one was afraid of it and backed off. I know you. I know you won't turn me down. But we're dealing with global power brokers, not back alley bookies."

I wasn't impressed. "So, you went to your Ivy Leaguers who were too chicken to get their hands dirty and after they soaked you and threw you overboard you came to me."

Roscoe sat on a corner of my desk like Humpty Dumpty. He fumbled a beat-up cigarette from a pocket, stuck it between his teeth, lit it with my desktop lighter. After the end glowed red, he drew one very deep drag, then stubbed out the butt. Natalie looked over at him. She examined his face and said, "Why am I even telling you this? You have no idea the scale of matters involved here. These are the CEOs of national sovereign central banks. They're European financial magnates."

Roscoe glanced at Carl Colossal, turned back to Natalie. The media maven presented an easy picture to study and he studied her, unabashedly. Finally, he exhaled a smoke screen in her general direction. He asked her, "You mean like Malcolm Rothberg? Of the Buckinghamshire Rothbergs? His family is worth trillions, and that welcher still owes me a grand a hole plus ten G's for the game. I whupped his ass at St. Andrews." He paused, then added, "That's 27 grand! I just hope he's one of those involved."

I asked, "Twenty-seven?"

"I let him win the first hole, of course." He paused, took another bite from his sandwich. "So, when do we leave for

Schutzenmattpark? You'll steer us in the right direction, make introductions, that kind of thing."

She stood and reached inside her black Hermes clutch. Her slender, hand-model fingers pulled out another pair of dark sunglasses, *sans* camera. She located a hanky as well and dabbed her nose as she said, "Oh, I'll be going to Schutzenmattpark, Mister Ritter. But not in your company, I'm afraid."

I said, "You're going to have to, Natalie. I'm occupied and Roscoe handles your kind of case. I can vouch for his results; and he's available immediately. Believe me, you're in good hands."

She pulled her shades down on her nose and gave him a prolonged once-over. She asked, "Do you even have a passport?"

Roscoe reached into the breast pocket of his suit. He removed a long red leather billfold, flashed his worn and beaten blue passport at Natalie. He said, "Speed costs money. How fast do you want to go?"

"I can afford it," she said. "Meet me at LaGuardia in two hours. My jet is waiting." She looked at me. "If he's late, you're fired."

"We'll base our fees on a percentage of the settlement," I said. "Five percent is standard. Roscoe?" I looked across at the human Dreamsickle for confirmation.

Natalie said, "Fine."

Roscoe intervened. He clasped palms with her in a sudden bimanual handshake. "Nine! Done! Great. Nine. You can afford it. See you at JFK."

Her face flushed with exasperation. "LaGuardia!" She looked over at me. "Nine percent? That's steep, but I'm desperate. OK. Nine."

My portly colleague from the bottom floor escorted the attractive media heiress and Carl Colossal toward our hallway exit. When they reached our double doors, Natalie spun and broke loose from Roscoe's arm. Her heels made staccato clacks as she stormed back to me in my office, got within an inch of my face. Her whisper wasn't a whisper. "We were at a Birknerhaus orgy and you blew me off. We could have had a lot of fun! And now, my entire empire is being pirated and you palm me off on some reject from *Columbo*?"

Roscoe returned and wedged himself into the doorway. "We'll have to fly into *EuroAirport Basel-Mulhouse-Freiburg* in Saint-Louis, France across the Swiss border. It's only five miles from the BGS headquarters in Schutzenmattpark on the Rhine; about 3,700 miles from here. What make is your airplane?"

The tone of disdain in Natalie's reply descended from the heights of Mount Condescension. She said, "It isn't a Sopwith Camel." She mocked his question: "What's your *airplane* ... My *private jet* is a 2017 Gulfstream G280."

"Good," said Roscoe. "We can fly non-stop. Your range is 4,100 miles. With an air speed of 500 we should be there in eight hours, 17 minutes. If we leave in a couple of hours, we can arrive for early breakfast."

I would have laughed, but the day was too long and I was too tired. I said to the alluring Miss Cocks, "Do you remember a couple of months ago, President Jackson's election campaign sued CCP News for defamation?"

"They settled out of court," she said.

I said, "Yes. For $16,000,000."

"What does that have to do with," she looked across at Roscoe. "Him?"

"That was his case," I said. "He proved the behind the scenes intent, produced their email trails they thought they deleted and covered up."

"Oh," she said. She smirked as I watched her hips saunter away. "Well, we'll see how he does up against the big boys. *Ciao.*"

15

Trouble

* * *

The rippling waves of the East River reflected the last rays of the setting sun when an Uber Black dropped me off at my warehouse on the waterfront side of FDR Drive. As I arrived a short moving van departed. I got out, spiffed my driver a fistful of cash, pushed through my three-inch steel front door.

Trouble came straight at me down the stairs from the second floor. The empty space behind her previously served as her artist's studio. My little sister received full scholarship offers from the School of the Museum of Fine Arts at Tufts University in Boston when she tested with a 161 IQ and posted near perfect SAT scores, but no dice.

Instead, she earned her BFA degree in Studio Art from Coker University in South Carolina. Her chosen alma mater's intimate student population of 1,100 was much more to her liking but the big reason was the freedom they provided to experiment with her artistic creativity.

Trouble Wolfe became a 21st-century, rapid-fire pointillist artist. Her Thompson .45 submachine gun was her brush, and its 50-round drum magazine contained her paints. Her palette provided but one color: lead gray.

On four-foot by five-foot steel plates, my little sister painted Native American Chiefs in full headdress from a distance of 25 feet. Her Chicago typewriter artwork stirred global controversy. Consequently, the price of her originals soared into the stratosphere.

And what a knockout. I know; this was My Little Sister, the same toe-headed kid in braces who blasted my father with a boisterous root-beer belch when he asked about her day at school. But she inherited the pulchritude of our family's genes, and Trouble grew into a natural voluptuous stunner. If you saw the two of us next to each other, me you'd want to kill, her you'd want to kill for.

Unlike Avalon's desire to remain inconspicuous in public, l'il sis enjoyed her notoriety. She was dressed to the nines. Josh Hitt's pupils were going to dilate when he watched her killer body, blonde hair, blue eyes, and million-dollar nose exit that plane.

Her destination was the home of a Hollywood actor who became an accidental friend. I met the action movie hero the year before when I burned down the Birknerhaus Hotel with the global pedophile trafficking cabal inside.

The movie star had handed me a Red Stripe beer as he, Electra, and I observed the flames and black smoke against the pink Caribbean sunrise. Against the dim light of dawn, we watched the annual meeting place and bacchanalia of the perverts get incinerated to perdition.

Josh got into Trouble at our White House wedding. And I mean literally. I walked by, heard my sister's voice, peeked into the ballroom coat closet–saw that she kept her entire fair complexion devoid of tattoos. Their scene was the whole adolescent cliché. The floor and feinting divan were covered with discarded clothes, none from the coat racks.

After our Honeymoon Train delivered us to San Antonio, the "romantically linked" pair of artists continued on toward Hollywoodland. When they learned about our 1,000 volunteers fighting at Alamo II, they made a 180-degree about-face and joined us. Josh saved my life twice with his movie-trained pistolero skills and Trouble, well, did we protect her or did she protect us?

As she carefully tread down the stairs, I chuckled at her precarious balance in a pair of black Jimmy Choos. But in her tight little black dress, every viewpoint I saw created ample distraction from her unsteady ambulation in cocktail footwear. My sister cradled her black and white Shih Tzu, Winston, in her arms. She said, "The limo will be here in a minute."

I couldn't help it. I didn't want to say it, but I was the big brother. I asked, "Are you sure about doing this? You're entering a very weird community of people."

She bypassed my question. "Josh has a big golf green at his house. I wanted to set up my studio outdoors, the air is so nice at his place in L.A."

I said, "The air? Los Angeles? Are we talking about the same place?"

"He's converting an underground bowling lane for me. Perfect shooting gallery."

"Isn't this just a little soon?" I asked.

"Soon? You married Electra six months after you met."

The grim downturn of my mouth didn't prevent me from responding. I said, "We went through a lot together. I rescued her boy from congressional pedophiles; we burned down the Birknerhaus Group in a shoot-em-up firefight. Those things create deep bonds, fast."

She said, "I guess defending the Alamo shoulder to shoulder against a foreign invasion and 40-to-1 odds isn't the same. Come on, Nick. The Prez is going to kiss you on the cheek on national TV for that. I'd be there, but Josh got me a line in his new movie." She tiptoed and kissed my cheek. "You're such a worry wart. I'll be fine. You know how Josh loves to shoot."

She laughed. "I might even be able to teach him how to hit something."

"He shot well enough in action," I said. "I don't know that he needs much coaching."

"Speaking of which, your wife's skills have advanced nicely, thank you very much. She's quick on the uptake."

"Great," I said. "You guys are nuts."

"What? Punching out pictures with a crossbow on heavy card stock? You should be happy. It takes her mind off of things. Like when Einstein played his violin."

I said, "A thousand square miles of south Texas ranches to run, plus the owner of White Petroleum, and the *Maison Blanche* here on Madison Avenue, and you get her to take up archery art."

Trouble smiled and said, "She loves it, says it's the most relaxing Zen experience she's had. It's painstaking compared to my Thompson, but she's already progressed past stick figures. She uses a repeating crossbow with a five-shot auto-loading magazine. That helps."

I said, "She's turned part of the fourth floor into a shooting gallery." I paused. I thought the whole thing was ridiculous, but who was I to judge? It made my wife happy. *And if mama ain't happy, ain't nobody happy.*

I said, "She says she hasn't figured out how to align her feathers for the right shading effects. What's up with that?"

After a slight laugh, Trouble said, "Her chiaroscuro isn't there yet. She'll get it. Just takes time and practice." She clutched Winston and scrunched up her face. A lot of ladies who took High Tea at The Palm would have paid a fortune to have that nose. "Come on, Nick. See me off at the airport."

For the second time in one afternoon, I turned down the company of a lovely member of the female persuasion. "I'm afraid you'll have to go alone," I said.

She pouted.

"You know," I said, "Jack."

"I don't know Jack," she said. "You're the one who knows Jack. What's he got to do with it?" She indicated the briefcase in my hand. "What's that?"

By then I had my 60-second summary of the day's events down pat and told her as the black airport town car pulled up at our door. Stunned, saddened, still, she wanted to make her flight to her future.

Our hug was deep and lasting. When I opened my eyes I was pulled from a profound unknown into the dusk of reality. The diminishing daylight painted my sister with surreal effects when she walked away, then sat in the car as the driver closed her door. The town car's taillights glowed in the impending nightfall as they quietly rolled away and vanished from sight. I turned to walk inside, briefcase in hand.

Fragments of masonry blew off my building's wall in front of my nose and peppered my face. I ducked, grabbed my .45s from its shoulder holster. A dumpster provided cover, but not before another silent shot exploded steel shrapnel from its side into my cheek.

16

Electra

* * *

Intuition shoved my hands upward and turned the briefcase into a shield before my face. Another shot knocked it from my grasp. It tumbled to the ground and stayed shut as it clattered across the pavement. Before it settled, I sprang out and scooped it up like a fumbled football as I bolted through my open front door. Another silent bullet followed, smashed into the doorframe.

I used the massive three-inch steel door as a bulletproof shield, slid behind it and slammed it shut. The ensuing silence signaled a cease-fire. I was safe inside; Cody was upstairs.

I bolted up two flights of steps and checked in with my sole remaining housemate, Cody the Cougar. His third-floor penthouse windows provided a 360-degree view of the area: over FDR Drive, across the East River, under the nearby overpass.

I swept the area with my 50X nautical binoculars–nothing. No reflections of rifle scopes or lenses. No cars, no boats. Nobody ran anywhere. I didn't see squadoosh.

I looked beside me. Cody's long, feline body stretched up to full length like a Slinky and stood at my side as he, too, peered out the window. He didn't see anything, either.

I debated, did the right thing and called it in. The dispatcher said they would have picked up the sound of the gunshots with their ShotSpotter technology. They said nothing showed up; they had other calls to get to. CLICK. So, because a Manhattan network of mic'd up drones didn't hear silenced shots fired on the banks of the East River, nothing happened. I told them to fuhgeddaboudit.

At the end of a very long Monday, I was tired. I was hungry. I needed a shower. I needed to sleep. I dropped my double crossbolts onto the door, set my indoor and outdoor security systems on high alert.

Electra picked up my call as I sat in Cody's penthouse suite on the third floor of my building. The mountain lion's purr resonated like a motorboat as his head rested in my lap. I slowly stroked his torso down his back to his thick bottlebrush tail and listened as Mom spoke.

Even in a state of irritation, the new Mrs. Wolfe could charm a thief into a confessional booth. "You've been in New York too long, Nick. You should have been here by now. Little Nick misses you so much. Please get back as early as you can tomorrow. It will be time to get across the street to the White House before you know it."

I said, "I'll catch the Northeast Regional to Union Station tomorrow."

"Please don't get hung up on anything," she said. "John's favorability rating skyrocketed after Alamo II. With the election coming up, the globalists would love to make a spectacle of anything to embarrass him and pull him down. He catches so much flak from this one-party press."

I said, "You don't have to be polite with me, baby. You know my word for them. I hate the bastards."

"Please, Nick."

"One more thing," I added. "I'm going to check Cody and me into the hotel in the morning to get us out of here before they repaint."

We matched, "I love you," sign offs. I said, "*Hasta manana,* baby," and clicked off our call. My thoughts left the Big Apple. In my mind's eye, I astro-soared to Washington, D.C. and looked through a window inside the White Mansion. I watched little Nick, and Preston's previous son, Horace, with the woman I loved.

A decade before, the tall, auburn-haired beauty who owned 650,000 acres of south Texas ranchland married fracking pioneer, Preston T. White and his thousands of square miles of north Texas oil leases. Their union drove a golden spike in the heart of Texas that multiplied their combined fortunes into the stratosphere. His sudden heart attack a few years later widowed her with the two boys.

When she popped the big question to me after my firefight on St. Thomas took down the international group of pedophiles, I was barely alive. I fought off hit men, bodyguards and a massive robot and lay crippled on the floor, bullwhipped by sadistic twins as the place burned around us. We got out alive by less than the skin of our teeth.

Six months later, we took our wedding party on a private honeymoon train to her McDonald Ranch HQ. But her phone rang, and we became embroiled in the defense of Joint Base San Antonio and the Texas southern border.

40,000 rogue Chinese, Hamas and Mexican cartel raiders stormed across on the morning of Memorial Day as an advance force before the freshly rebuilt Mexican Army. It became a family affair when Electra fired an M-60 from the south wall, Trouble saved the life of Brigadier General Rhys Willoughby with her Thompson paint brush, and Josh Hitt saved mine with his silver screen instinct shooting. Twice.

At Alamo II, my five-foot-ten-inch, 123-pound wife and lady of finishing-school refinement and poise looked hotter than ghost peppers, and not in a little black sequined cocktail dress. The elegant lady who was often flash photographed for the society pages cradled an M60 machine gun in the crook of her arm in khaki fatigues. She piloted her helicopter and addressed the international terrorists in fluent 7.62 x 51 millimeter NATO-speak.

She was right. I needed to get back to D.C. I wasn't crazy about the land of bureaucrats, but my wife, my family, plus FLOTUS and POTUS with his Medal of Freedom, all called. *Dammit.*

As soon as I wrapped up one nagging question, I would see them all again. I looked at the briefcase. *What's inside this damned thing?*

17

Briefcase

* * *

Three guys were at Jack's the morning he died; dozens more from the gym were his friends. On Saturday afternoons any random collection of us gathered for pow-wows in his office. While we smoked cigars and scratched off lottery cards, we argued about economics, politics, and who would have won a real one-on-one between Magic and Bird. As gorgeous models and their photographers departed down the creaky steps from their Saturday morning photo shoots, we flashed our scorecards. Every one of us held up a ten.

Similar to the descent of the smoothly muscled photogenic felines down Jack's aged staircase, Cody padded beside me downstairs from his penthouse to Trouble's empty shooting studio. The heavy briefcase lay where I parked it on the floor. I lifted it and laid it on top of a lonely lateral file cabinet.

My phone rang. I picked it up.

"Nick?"

"Who's this?"

"Nick Wolfe?"

The voice sounded familiar, but I had trouble placing it over the phone.

"This' Jet. See me tomorrow morning. At the gym. About Jack."

I said, "Jet, I have to catch a train ..."

CLICK.

After that prolonged philosophical discussion, I opened Trouble's oversized dorm fridge. The ice cold Miller High Life bottle was just what I needed. I rolled it's damp barrel across my brow. Her junk drawer coughed up a couple of cancer sticks that weren't too mangled. The beer's taste refreshed me, but not as much as the wet coolness of the bottle on my forehead in ninety-four degrees and 75% humidity. My place was big, empty, quiet.

Jack's oxblood briefcase stared at me. I slid the junk drawer open again to find my lock picks. Then I remembered the lottery card that was attached to the pawn ticket and the circled numbers on it: 52 and 25. I looked at the gold-plated latches and tumblers. Four digits, 5. 2. 2. 5. – j.a.c.k. The latches snapped open from the release of their springs.

The first thing I noticed when I opened it were the bullet dents. Only one slug struck the scratched-up case in my hands. There were an additional two dents on the same side. Not much short of a bazooka would have penetrated its three-quarter inch titanium structure. The once-smooth leather hid the other two battle scars beneath its elegant maroon surface.

Custom cut foam that filled the inside barely left room for its contents, with incisions that secured data sheets, photos, biographies, thumb drives and CDs. I looked over some of the papers because they were the easiest to see first. Through bleary eyes, I read European names I didn't recognize, saw ballistics data, trajectories, mapped distances, airborne security measures, nautical security options. Then there were the electronic pieces.

The night became so late it was early. I was too tired to make a deep dive into a bunch of statistical data. When I awoke, my face was cradled in my hands. I wiped my lips with a paper towel from the roll on Trouble's studio counter.

Cody and I shared some Las Vegas late night, early morning *nosh* and turned in.

* * *

When I got started the next morning, I booked Bellevue Property Restoration to scour and paint Trouble's bullet-ridden studio. Cody and I needed to move out for a week to avoid the fumes from muriatic acid used to strip the old paint, then the oil base paint that would follow. It also wouldn't hurt to move to a safe house while someone was trying to kill me.

Electra booked herself and the boys into the penthouse suite of her *Maison Blanche* hotel on Madison Avenue during the week leading up to New York's celebration of our nation's sestercentennial. With Trouble and Winston gone, it would provide discreet safe house living for Cody the Cougar and me.

After last night's gunshots knocked on my front door, I called our friends at Impervious to provide local transportation. The high-security company for executives was staffed with former Spetsnaz professionals and worked with me on other cases. Valeriy Bubka was comfortable with Cody from my previous escapades and arrived in a black Range Rover Sentinel.

The 10,000 pound armored SUV had 510 horsepower and could survive a 33-pound bomb beside it, stop an AK-47 armor-piercing round with two inches of glass and polycarbonate, and only require me to turn up the volume of its stereo's 256 speaker sound system.

I checked Cody into the two-floor penthouse, where he climbed up to sleep on the hunter green suede sofa. Then I emptied the briefcase contents into a tray in the *Maison Blanche* safe until I returned and could delve into it in depth.

I had to assume that whoever was after me might have my daily behavior plotted with a traffic pattern. *Damn. When did I start slipping?* I needed to push the Pause button on the clutter that swirled within my head. I had to concentrate, invoke my countersurveillance tradecraft, for Jack's case and for my life.

I carried the empty Article of Great Interest out to Valeriy's black Sentinel. After he drove us back to my part of town I secured the briefcase on Trouble's second floor. When I exited my place, my hands were empty. I had him drop me off at the Metro Diner and cut him loose. This was something I had to do alone.

The little hand was on the nine when I slid across the worn burgundy vinyl seat in my back corner booth. After my two-by-four breakfast of eggs, bacon, sausage and pancakes with toast and black coffee, I embarked on a mission.

Spy *vs* Spy

"See" is the operative word in counter-surveillance and I had to see if I was being surveilled. My adversary could not lose sight of me for one millisecond. My job was to see *him*. I'd find a predetermined position where I could spot someone for a second time without being made, myself. Then I'd lead them there by convoluted routes that could trip them up into exposing themselves without giving them anything concrete from me.

Outside the Metro's door, I quickly reconsidered the flavor of my coffee and decided I needed one last impromptu sip. I went inside, leaned over the table, did not look outside the window, picked up my cup. I don't remember if I tasted it.

I hoofed it on a meandering route for a couple of blocks with a visit into a men's shoe store, then a post office. I tested the fluidity of Mont Blanc pens in one setting, then was almost asphyxiated by the intense luscious aroma inside a leather haberdashery. Nope. One pay phone still existed in the Lower East Side at an inconspicuous intersection. From that position, I could pick up anyone in several directions behind me. I stepped up and dropped coins in the slot. Nobody.

*　*　*

I squeaked up the stairs at Jack's Gym. All morning long I maintained a keen vigil for a surreptitious tail and came up blank. Despite my intense awareness of my surroundings, I was caught off guard by the vision that descended in the semi-dark above me.

Avalon's slow-motion approach down the rough staircase in a snatched mini dress paused time and space in the musty void that surrounded us. The international runway phenomenon looked like she stepped out of a glossy photo on Jack's Wall of Fame and onto the staircase landing a few steps ahead.

Her slender ankles grew upward into a mannequin's perfect calves and curvaceous, long, three-point legs that climbed to slim, bikini-friendly hips. The skin-tight pink fabric squeezed an anorexic waist that ascended into pronounced pointed breasts, and softly tanned bare shoulders that made you want to grasp them and pull her forward into your arms.

In the dim light, the limbal rings around her striking irises thinned as her pupils enlarged and, once again, she read my mind. She smiled. In her seductive accent she said, "I will remember to dress incognito less often. *Oui?*"

My early-morning gravel tone didn't come out as the gracious welcome I intended. "What are you doing here?" I asked.

She stopped one step above mine. On the stair above the one on which she stood, she set down a white Hermes Kelly bag. In a soft, smooth motion she placed her hands on my shoulders. The glamor model leaned forward and allowed her generous cleavage to spill open before my eyes. When she spoke, her soft, warm breath flowed over my ear, then down my neck beneath my collar. "This is where I come to find a rough, rugged man."

She pulled back, read my face. "You are still upset," she said.

"I'm here to meet a guy about Jack before I catch a train to D.C. What are you doing here?"

Her face registered her disappointment. "My locker," she said. "You removed your *equipement*. The police released their hold on the crime scene for me." She picked up her Kelly bag and dangled it before me with a smile.

I'll bet they did. If Avalon had asked, Ali Baba would have personally rolled open his cave door for her. I let out a deep breath and spoke through a grimace. "Sorry. I've got a one-track mind."

"I wish," she said with her customary two ee's in *wish*. "So do I, darling." She resumed her walk down the long staircase.

If a lady's legs look good in flats, they become awesome in heels. Hers were awesome in flats. And she knew I watched her take each, and every, tantalizing step. Those legs were gifts from God to the visions of the men of earth. Her lithe body emitted a negative magnetic charge that fired an electrostatic attraction at the positive ions of the male species.

At the bottom she stopped, turned back toward me. She held the glass door open and said, "In your American music they say ..." She paused again, acted like she was thinking when she cocked her head and touched her temple with the tip of her index finger. "Wait, I am saying it wrong sometimes." She looked up at me with a smile and winked. "A good man, *ees* hard to find. *Au revoir!*"

She waved, spun on one heel and stepped out the door and onto the sidewalk. I heard a horn honk, a dog bark, a screech of tires from slammed brakes, followed by the frightening sound of crunching metal, glass and rubber.

18

Jet

* * *

When I got to the top of the stairs Jack's register book was gone, replaced by a duty cop in a chair. He looked around me down the stairs for his own parting glimpse of the supermodel. He said, "She's somethin' else, huh?"

"Yeah," I said. "I'm meeting my sparring partner. She said you lifted the crime scene?"

He looked at his watch. "She just wanted her stuff. It was only ten minutes early."

I looked at him and grinned. "I'm sure you helped her with it, too."

"Yeah, well, you know," he said. Then, "Hey, wait a minute!"

"Calm down," I said. "Just joking. Who wouldn't, right?"

With that, he relaxed. We talked a few minutes until I heard Jet's recognizable heavy, thudding, clodhoppers as he trudged up the stairs. Bill "Jet" Wilson had been a prize fighter who carried his Olympic bronze medal in the pocket of whatever pants he wore. Much more than a sparring partner, he gave me insight to fighting I got from nobody else. One of the most valuable lessons I took away after years of boxing with Jet was,

Never Fight a Fighter

You may be an incredible athlete: you lift a lot of weight, you shoot a ball through a hoop, you hit a pitched baseball, you charge the offensive line. He doesn't do any of those things. It doesn't matter. You're not a fighter. That's all he does. Fight. He will take you apart, because that is what he does. He takes people apart. He pummels people into oblivion for a living. He knows 15 pressure points that can cripple you. You're 6'6" and 300 pounds and he's only 5'11" and 210? He will destroy you. Never fight a fighter.

My boxing coach may not have been a ballet star climbing the stairs, but when Jet stepped into the ring it was easier to find a ghost. He looked at me out of the corner of his eye, greeted me with, "Nick."

"Hi, Jet."

He pointed ahead. "In the ring," he said.

I felt out of place when I climbed between the ropes in my street clothes. Jet walked to one corner, took a seat on the stool.

"Glad you called, Jet. What's up?"

He sat. He looked from side to side, rubbed his hands together. "It's, gimme a minute."

"Don't worry about me, Jet. I'm your pal. But I've got a train to catch."

He dropped his head, muttered, "Only you, Nick. You're the only one." The former "Missouri Mauler" reached outside the ring. His hands rummaged through a nearby equipment box. He returned his attention inside the ring when he found what he wanted.

"I just, I don't know," he said. "I know it was somethin', but it was more than just somethin'."

His feet slid inside a pair of boxing shoes that came out of the box and cinched their laces tight around his ankles. He looped one end of yellow hand wrap around his thumb, wound it in and out and around his fingers, then out and around his knuckles, securing it over the top with white athletic tape. He cradled a pair of red bag gloves in his lap, slid one on, then tugged at the other one with his teeth. I helped push it onto his massive mitt.

Jet rose from the tripod stool and took the center of the ring. The guy had to be 50 if he was a day, but his motions and musculature were smooth and precise, far superior to the wild passions of an overzealous young fighter. He slowly moved about: jabbed, ducked, crossed.

As he launched a couple of warm-up combinations at his shadow, he said, "You know how he's always holdin' court in his office. It was early last week. He had that guy in there, you know, with the *Daily Mirror*."

"Scoop."

"Yeah–Scoop."

I nodded. Scoop wasn't my favorite guy. Reporters and I were as compatible as fire and ice.

"They's always arguin' about somethin'. Ali, Marciano, Tyson, you know."

Another nod of agreement.

"This was different. They'd argue, they'd fight, they'd break out laughin' the same way. But it wasn't about fighters." Jet stopped his shadow boxing motions, looked around the empty gym, drew in close. He said, "Jack told Scoop and Jack brought the receipts. I saw them in there, lookin' hard at some stuff. Scoop just whistled and sat back in his chair."

"What were they arguing about?"

"Murders. Assassinations. Jack had the goods on everybody. On everything. They was talkin' about the shots they just fired on Jackson. He went through all the JFK shooters, then the CIA hit man that shot RFK in the back. Not Sirhan. Sirhan stood in front of RFK. The kill shot came from a couple of inches behind him. And then MLK, and then Malcolm X and Fred Hampton. He showed that guy everything. Jack named

Who's Who in the Zoo, man! That sweet old dude had his act together, man."

I listened, said, "I doubt if a hack for the *Mirror* killed Jack because of that."

"Not that," he said. "This." Jet climbed through the ring ropes. He walked into Jack's office, beckoned me with a wave of his red-gloved hand as I followed him in. He pointed at the desk, as much as he could wearing sixteen-ounce leather fist protection. "Wait a minute!" he said. "It's gone. It's all gone."

I walked in beside him. "What's gone?"

"He had all kinds of stuff laid out here," said Jet. "A map, big map. Upper New York Bay and the Hudson River around The Battery and Governor's Island. Photos of Liberty Island, Ellis Island. There were big red marker lines drawn from point to point across the Hudson and everything. He had books out, binders."

The only diagrams on top of his desk for our eyes to see were outlines of Jack's body, with aluminum fingerprint powder residues from the crime scene. I said, "I imagine the police took it in as evidence."

Jet said, "Jack told Scoop he had everything on the shooting last week in Pennsylvania. He knew who set it up. He had T.H.E. names from the top down. They argued. Jack said the FBI and Secret Service Directors were in cahoots, but they were just pawns. Then I heard him say he knew who financed that plus the second shooter attempt in Florida."

I hated politics and stayed away as far as possible from them. It was our nation's sestercentennial; it was an election year; and I was happy to stay out of the whole thing. President Jackson was beloved by his base and supporters, but his communist opposition was extreme, militant, and violent.

Jack told me they did anything to gain power, maintain power, and never relinquish it once they had it. Including assassinations. They were globalist totalitarians that murdered their own to cover their tracks and advance their power positions. Human life was meaningless to them. Prior to President Jackson's current term, our nation had descended into George Orwell's *Animal Farm*.

Congress and the media harassed the president to an outrageous degree. They impeached him twice with bogus charges that didn't hold up. They filed ninety-one lawsuits against him for charges that weren't revealed, just to keep him in court and off the campaign trail during the upcoming election.

They accused him of being Hitler, of being "an existential threat to democracy." The previous president told the national news media, "somebody should put a bullseye on him." The Speaker of the House told the media, "To make sure he never steps foot in the White House again."

They did everything they could from safe positions behind their teleprompters, to incite some poor deluded patsy into a rage of assassination. And in the last four weeks, two presidential murder attempts narrowly failed.

The night before, I was beyond tired when Pandora nudged me to open Jack's heavy metal luggage. I opened, I saw, I slept. After listening to Jet, I realized why it was bulletproof titanium and hidden away. The old guy had mapped out the first two assassination attempts on President Jackson, in Pennsylvania and Florida. Was he calculating the third?

The shelves that sagged behind Jack's desk held his and his brother's forensic investigations. Binders of data and photos showed everything on JFK, RFK, MLK, *et al* that Congress didn't want to see, the evidence they were warned against pursuing. As it did so effectively with the assassinations of the 60s, the Deep State covered up the first two new millennium attempted murders of the president.

I thanked Jet. I was tight on time to catch my train.

19

Scoop

* * *

Nicknames are a funny phenomenon. When somebody gets tagged with a good one, it becomes their identity. People forget their actual name; from that moment forward their name becomes their nickname. In his case, the handle we hung on the hack that called himself a journalist was Scoop.

I knew where to find him on the way to my train. Since the global planned-demic China virus locked people out of their workplace offices, most of his ilk, like thousands of government workers, maintained their jobs from their homes as long as they could. When I identified myself after his peephole lens darkened, he opened his door.

Scoop's heavy-lidded eyes peered out from a tired face that wore three days of stubble, above a coffee-stained T-shirt and checkerboard black and white felt pajama bottoms. His rooster-like bed hair peaked on the middle of his head. The words that passed over his chicken lips were preceded by a mouthful of super-cala-frag-alistic-extra-halitosis. He said, "You couldn't have called?"

I checked my watch. "I've got to catch a train," I said. "I don't have time for small talk." I pushed my way past him into his place.

As I passed by him, his breath smelled even worse. "Nice to see you too, Wolfe."

"Tell me about your talk with Jack last week. All of it."

"Screw you," he said. The worn fabric of a green sleeper sofa in a corner of the room revealed the foam of its cushions. He took a seat, said, "First of all, freedom of the press means I don't have to tell you anything. Second, don't come into my home and tell me what to do. Screw you, Wolfe. Go play tough guy somewheres else."

I walked to his outside window and looked down. It was a funny situation, loaded with comic potential. I took a seat next to him on his couch, reached into a pocket. "You know, Scoop," I said, "Jack was a personal friend, more than just a guy that owned a gym."

He sat still in silence, eyed me with suspicion.

I said, "The police are investigating his murder."

His shock seemed genuine. "I heard he died but that's all I know. Murder?"

"About 24 hours ago," I said. I found my pack of cigs, knocked one loose. "Right now, he's on a slab in the morgue. Somebody shivved him in his back at his desk."

Scoop didn't move, still silent. I clinked my lighter open and ratcheted its wheel, lit up. "I'm going to nail his killer but I've got to catch a train to D.C. so the president can hand me a people's hero medal. I need you to tell me what went on in Jack's office. Now."

He protested the smoke from my cigarette. "Hey! Who said you could smoke in my house!"

While my eyes held his in a steadfast stare, I stubbed out the butt on the back of my left hand. The red coals of its lit end burned my flesh until it expired into black ash and smoke. I didn't enjoy the experience, burning flesh stinks.

He smirked. "If you're trying to do a one man show as both good cop and bad cop, you're getting two thumbs down."

* * *

Scoop's apartment in the Lower East Side featured pane glass windows that opened outward. Each of my hands gripped one of his ankles. Four floors beneath his scalp and dandruff, the wet sidewalk glistened in the sporadic sunlight. The alleged journalist screamed for help, gulped for air, bawled some more. A TV remote and his mobile phone fell from his PJ pockets in slow motion and exploded on the sidewalk below.

My incisors bit down on the filter of my extinguished cigarette. Through clenched jaws I said, "Sound travels upward, you moron, not down." He flailed his arms and squawked how I couldn't do this, this was America, he had rights, freedom of the press, yadda, yadda, yadda. I let him feel my grip slip. "Oops!"

A minute later I hauled him back in. He sat in a chair by the window and trembled, couldn't hold his hands still. His pajama top was wet with his piss. "Shit, Wolfe, when I tell the cops about this they'll yank your license."

I lit a fresh cigarette, asked, "You want to go for round two?"

He threw his hands up in defense. "No! No!" he said. "Just, give me a minute."

I gave him five. A long five. What I learned in that short time would shake the world.

20

Shanghai

* * *

When Scoop opened his mind and his mouth, I almost drowned under the flood of information that poured out. The reporter described a scene I knew well: Jack's office shelves that sagged under the weight of his books and binders. Scoop said Jack gave him the full presentation on the JFK assassination.

He saw the letters from the attorney for Billy Sol Estes to the DOJ. From his deathbed, the friend of LBJ volunteered to testify with the entire story behind the JFK assassination, plus a laundry list of other murders. Scoop saw the names, backgrounds, and firing positions of each of the six triggermen in Dealey Plaza that shot JFK. I remembered when I sat in the same office and received the same education.

As young men, Jack and Sam provided substantial evidence to the 1976 House Select Committee on Assassinations. The committee concluded that the JFK assassination was indeed a conspiracy and not a lone shooter. Then everybody went to lunch and swept it under the rug and it was all forgotten.

The brothers' efforts to bring attention to their additional murder cases were met in Washington by typical bureaucratic stonewalling and denial. Over drinks at the Capitol Grille with a man who referred to himself only as, "Son of Deep Throat," they were warned that they were sending up dangerous flares about themselves. It was a good way to get killed. So, they kept quiet about their work and increased the forensics on their findings for years as their personal labors of love. Now, with the advent of global social media and independent journalism, they were ready to spring their evidence loose for worldwide view.

He told me Jack also pulled a dedicated "9-11" binder down and flopped it open on his desk. Its contents showed Scoop forensic evidence of the traitors who were behind the inside job of September 11th. With names. The Secretary of State was on video a few days before, saying the government had misplaced 2.7 trillion dollars for which it could not account. Then the site that housed all of our financial information, Building Seven, collapsed.

Scoop said, "You know, you only have to ask a few basic questions. Nano particles of aluminum and iron were present, both used to make thermite bombs in the World Trade Centers and Building Seven. How did the molten steel happen if the burn temperature of aircraft fuel isn't hot enough to do that? How did all those phone calls to homes and offices get made when cell phones did not operate above 5,000 feet in 2001? Enlarged photos showed military drones were used, not commercial airliners. Why was there zero airplane wreckage at the Pentagon? Why were its grounds completely covered over and buried immediately after?

Scoop said that's when Jack brought their arguments around to more current events. He pulled out his data about both recent attempts on President Jackson's life.

The attempted shooting of the president at a campaign event in Pennsylvania was overseen by several government three-letter department heads. Coincidentally, that event happened to be the *only* campaign rally of the entire election season that Jackson's political foes on the CCP TV network selected to televise live.

What I heard next peaked my interest. Jack believed he had a line on the money men, the ones that paid for the subversive activities. One lead was the SEC's complete, unabridged stock exchange report for Friday, the day before the Pennsylvania shooting on Saturday, that included an investment firm in Texas.

Scoop said that Friday, the day before President Jackson was shot in the head and survived assassination by a millimeter, they put in a massive, short position against his family business with the stock ticker JTJ.

If the president had been killed, the stock would have plummeted. Their massive, short position would have profited nearly a trillion dollars. Instead, because of a one millimeter head turn, they owed millions in margin calls for their ill-timed Put.

Then!

In an amazing piece of United States stock exchange history, something happened that never occurred since it opened in 1790. The SEC mysteriously allowed the $12,000,000 of Puts made by the firm to be erased from their records the next day after the hit didn't go down as planned. No margin calls. The explanation? "It was a mistake, a glitch."

Scoop said, "That's when Jack said, 'So, if you or I took out a short sell position on a company and it went north instead of south, do you think the SEC would allow us to just say, 'Oops! My bad!' and forget about the whole thing? On a $12,000,000 Put?"

That took serious, Serious, S.E.R.I.O.U.S. money and influence. That took global power. Jack had the names of the principle investors in the firm, a former president, former vice president, the Rothbergs, SlickRock Corporation, and their connections to international sovereign central banks.

That was what I wanted. Names. I hated dealing with collective group theories, but I was pretty successful when I worked *mano a mano*. To identify the culprits, Jack followed my procedural rules of investigating any crime:

1) Whenever in doubt, always look for the financial incentive.

1a) Who stands to gain?

2) It's always an inside job.

When I played by that strategy, I was right 90% of the time.

Jack told Scoop he had all his evidence and data secured where nobody could get it. Days later, he was killed. Scoop was too incompetent to find Jack's stash and get his hands on it for his own use. He would have been dead before I ever saw him if he had tried. But what if Scoop tipped off the wrong people?

I may have picked up the bad guys' game plan playbook in the bulletproof briefcase Jack passed to me in secret. That meant I was carrying the nuclear football. Four shots just missed me. Whoever *they* were, they wanted to get it, or to get me, probably both. *What the Hell was in it?*

Fortunately, I stashed its contents in a safe location away from my home until my return. I said, "Did you put this out anywhere? In the *Mirror*?"

"Well, maybe, a little."

"What!"

"It's good stuff, Nick. My editors went crazy over it."

I wanted to slug him. I wanted to hang him out of his window again. I counted to ten, then experienced a crashing epiphany. *What I want, my end game, is Jack's killer. As long as he knows I possess the information he wants, he has to go through me to get it. I need to go into 360-degree surveillance mode. The only way to take him out is to draw him out.*

I patted his shoulder and said, "Scoop, when I get back I'll buy you a round."

He looked at me through agonized eyes. "Don't bother," he said. "I don't like to drink upside down."

I needed to make tracks if I was going to catch the train to D.C. A passing hack pulled over when I flagged him down. I told him I didn't want some polite online livery service; I needed crosstown street level speed, *pronto*. I spiffed him a Grant and climbed in the back. Ulysses' friendly face on the bill encouraged the Bolshevik cabbie and he whipped his horsepower like Santa Claus at dawn with gifts to deliver. When he made hard turns I slid side to side across the dark flat vinyl of the bench back seat.

A flash bulletin cut into his local radio program. The owner of a decades old pawn shop in Two Bridges was killed in his shop. The place was tossed.

We hustled up to 7th Avenue and West 31st Street. I jumped out across from Madison Square Garden, tipped my Formula One cab driver with another Grant. I checked my watch, still had half an hour to make my train. I was amazed; I should have gotten that cabby's phone number for future reference.

It was a busy morning in Midtown before the big holiday weekend. A crowd congested the entrance, and too many Fourth of July tourists and vacationers packed the down escalator for me to rush ahead to the All Trains level.

The pharmacy, the coffee shops and the book stores were all packed with travelers. I saw a shoe repair shop ahead on my right. Empty. I took advantage of my new time cushion and the conspicuous vacancy and ducked in for some quick shoe polish.

The shop was empty. The shine booth was empty. The place was devoid of human life, not one soul. That should have told me something. I should have picked up on it.

The next thing I knew, I hung upside down like a side of beef, in the dark, in a large cold space.

21

Voice

* * *

I looked upward past my heels. My feet were clamped together, bound by shackles that suspended me. My head hung above a concrete floor, and a steel cable stretched down to my ankles, taut from a support somewhere overhead in the darkness. The sharp pain in the skin of my wrists behind my back could only have been caused by zip ties.

"Thank you for joining us, *Herr* Wolfe," said a ubiquitous voice. "We have looked forward to our meeting."

I was as discombobulated as if I looked up from inside a tornado. Whatever it was that hit me, I wasn't alert enough to be angry. Yet. I growled, "Give me my boots. I've got a train to catch."

The voice that echoed from nowhere spoke through a scrambler. Even with the voice modulator, a Germanic accent showed through. It replied, "We are pressed for time as well. We have questions."

I said, "I have an answer. Get your estate plans in order."

The scrambled voice spoke again. "Threats, *Herr* Wolfe? The penchant of Nick Wolfe for violence is well documented. Fortunately, we are the parties who are the threat-ors; you are merely the threat-ee. Your arsenal is preposterous: a double barreled pistol? That *wenig* snub nose, and your pocket double-barreled shotgun? Most amusing."

I said, "My derringer. Cut me down and I'll show you how I shot jackrabbits on the hop when I was ten."

To my surprise, I heard the whine of an electric winch as I felt myself lowered toward the floor. The voice said, "Double-barreled pistols and shotguns. It appears you like things twice, *Herr* Wolfe."

When my head reached a foot above the deck, my downward motion stopped. An instant later, my crown smashed into the concrete floor when I was dropped onto my head. I felt myself winched upward again. The cuffs around my ankles clicked; my feet fell free. I crashed hard onto the cement again, tumbled over in a crumpled heap.

"Perhaps that is more to your liking, mister private investigator. Mister, agent of F.L.O.T.U.S."

* * *

I was disappointed by the amateurish look of surprise I felt cross my features.

Whoever it was, they were deep in the inner circle. F.L.O.T.U.S. was the all civilian, non-government Federal Lethal Operations Team of the United States run by the First Lady from the White House Deep Underground Command Center.

The voice addressed me again. "We know you are a Musketeer in the service of your Queen. For instance, that fashion backward pendant of hers that you wear. It died an unfortunate death–by *vorschlaghammer*."

F.L.O.T.U.S.

We didn't operate under Title 10; we didn't operate under Title 50; we weren't Title Anything. We were "confidential human resources," civilians who acted of our own volition, with White House patronage and collaboration. We were confidential human resources: extremely confidential, exceptionally resourceful.

Yvonne Jackson personally selected each of us; she supported our independent cases and causes because they aligned with hers. And we completed tasks in ways nobody else could. I was added as only the ninth independent member and each of us did whatever it took to get the job done, our own way.

The white amulet they destroyed was my Triad, a sophisticated device issued by the First Lady to her F.L.O.T.U.S. operators. It provided me with White House top secret clearance on any military installation or government office. When I pressed the red button at its center it instantly alerted the White House of my GPS location. The button itself injected a dose of Meth Adrenaline Delta 9 into my fingertip, turned me into Superman for 30 minutes. Or, it used to.

The voice said, "We both have important things to attend to. Yours is this afternoon in Washington, is it not?"

I had enough cloak and dagger. I wasn't crazy about using my Triad, but I was attached to it. It was handed to me personally by our First Lady. At that moment, I wanted it, and I wanted it badly. With its injection, I could have busted my bonds and released my inner silverback gorilla on the bastards. I hoped its GPS was triggered when they gave it the smash.

The attitude of retribution in my voice was difficult to control. "I'm bored. Kill me or cut me loose. I've got things to do, places to go, people to kill."

I heard a laugh in the background, then another. A pair of scrambled voices squabbled with bemusement. "We have no desire to kill you or cause you harm, *Herr* Wolfe. But we need to know what you know. Provide us with what you have from Jack."

They didn't buy the sweetness in my voice when I spoke. I said, "Cut me loose and I'll give you everything I've got."

The voice softened into a mocking tone. "Americans. We offer our hospitality, yet your attitude is ..." It paused. "Vituperative."

I rolled on the floor, tried to slip the zip ties that cut into my flesh. There was no way out; I was hog tied. The next words echoed throughout the limbo that was my expansive torture chamber. "Please, Mister Wolfe, relax. A drink, perhaps?"

A door opened on one side of the room and white light burned my eyes through the pitch black. Whoever crossed the hard floor was dressed head to foot in unmarked black face and body garb. Their crepe soles didn't make a sound.

I was rolled onto my back. Then came the Scotch, a lot of Scotch. Waves of it crashed into my mouth, against my compressed lips, across my face and head. The voice said, "This is the best single malt Scotch in the city; from Lafayette Street."

The Shadow above me forced more whiskey down my gullet. When I resisted with tightened lips and turns of my head, they splashed it across me and my clothes. I said, "I don't always drink whiskey, but when I do, I prefer Jim Beam."

The voice from everywhere said, "Seriously, *Herr* Wolfe. All we want is what your friend gave you."

Our charming *tete a tete* continued for hours. By the time they finished whiskey boarding the six-figure Scotch into me, onto me and over me, I didn't remember much. Frankly speaking, I didn't care much either.

That was OK; they had another bottle. I had whiskey in my hair, in my ears, my brain, my body, my clothes, my shoes. I didn't perspire; I oozed 50-year-old Macallan and my Scotch pressure was probably 300 over 190.

My hosts intensified their desire to obtain what I had. I felt sick, passed out. When I came around the voice sounded blurry. Hell, everything was blurry. I picked up a note of frustration in its intonation, then made out some words: "Inject," and "cocaine."

I felt someone grab my arm. I knew they were doing something to me, but my senses were shot. I only felt major motions, not fine responses like a needle that punctured my skin. In a rush I felt better, faster, more lucid. I wanted to talk—a lot. But my words were still garbled. I smelled like a distillery.

Distant banging on a door across the dark chamber interrupted their interrogation. Muffled voices behind the doors argued. Powerful pounding sounded again.

The questions ceased. In my new state of drug induced awareness, I listened with as much intensity as I could muster. The sound of footsteps dampened by soft soles ran toward me across the floor. Two hands gripped my torso, rolled me over onto my stomach.

My head was yanked up off the concrete by my hair. The razor-sharp edge of a blade touched my throat. The person that held my life in their hands said in a dispassionate, muffled voice, "Kill him?"

22

Gutter

* * *

From a hurried hot-mic discussion behind the scene, I heard a voice say something familiar, but out of place. It was something I might hear in a social conversation, but never in an interrogation. The voice was scrambled, but it was something they said, something I knew. Something my mind fought to recognize.

"No," came the scrambled response. "Bring him. Alive." My would-be nemesis tried to lift me. I felt hands grip my ankles, then two people dragged me across the floor.

As a rumbling jackshaft raised a garage door, a truck roared up, squeaking its tires as it stopped beside me on the smooth concrete floor. The wall of white sunlight that split the darkness when the overhead door opened hit my eyes hard and screwed my pupils down tight. I was tossed inside the cargo box like a smart TV, about to become another street hustle product that "just fell off the truck."

We turned, we braked, we slammed ahead. Every motion of the vehicle increased my feelings of inebriated nausea. At the apex of a quick left turn, I was shoved out the back into the gutter.

I tumbled a couple of times, my head banged off the curb. When I stopped bouncing and came to rest, my cheek lay on the concrete. The cement felt warm on my face and I turned my head to pass out. Above the sounds of street traffic, I heard the voices of people who walked by on the sidewalk. Their comments weren't nice. Several people watched me through their cameras. *The heat feels good. I like the heat. I'm glad it isn't Christmas. That would be cold. Wait, of course it isn't Christmas. WTF? Christmas?*

They must have cut my zip ties because I found that I had my hands again. When I tried to stand, I pitched forward into a parked car. I found a street sign, pulled myself up hand-over-hand and climbed until I stood in a vertical position. I was hammered–a walking, stumbling distillery that perspired the scent of booze.

It was hard enough to think of anything that made sense, much less speak. As much as I tried to do something, say something, I couldn't manage functional words or actions of any kind. Nobody stopped. People avoided me like it was 2020 and I didn't wear a mask. All around me, onlookers recorded videos on their phones.

Each step I took resembled the first new movements of an injured person in rehab. With my herkie jerky locomotion, I managed to make it across the sidewalk to a storefront's glass display window. I leaned against it and looked outward. I found myself muttering through thick lips, "Where am I?" It was all one big blur.

A hand gripped one of my shoulders. Its dark, uniformed companion said, "You're on Madison Avenue, pal. Where'd you think you were?" I looked to my side. I thought I saw a man, and he looked like he wore blue. *Am I on stage with The Blue Man Group? How did I get here?*

With my clearest elocution and enunciation, I was certain that I asked him, *"Hey! Blue Men! Aren't you guys playing at Astor Place? Why don't you ever say anything? You ought to try singing."*

His reply didn't make sense. He said, "Call me Little Boy Blue again mister, and we're gonna have a problem. Come on; you need some sleepy time and a meal. I'm taking you in."

That isn't what I said!

A marquee of lights above me flashed in my brain; their message snapped my mind into a temporary lucidity. In a startling moment of *non-sequitur* composure I said, "Yes, officer. I am going in. To my penthouse suite." I pointed skyward along the lines of the tall building. "Up there."

We elevated our eyes in slow tandem. The 500 white light bulbs overhead proclaimed, *Maison Blanche*. I was at the front entrance to Electra's White Hotel on Madison Avenue.

He replied, "Sure you are. And we have your private limousine right over here." I took a moment and composed my speech. It was obvious he was having difficulty comprehending what I was saying. I needed everything to come out with clarity.

I was conscientious to keep my details straight. My brain told me that what I said to the member of New York's Finest was this: "This is *my* hotel. And when I say, 'my hotel' I mean, I own it. Or, my wife does. You see, she's Electra White, but we got married so now she's Electra Wolfe. She was Electra McDonald, see, but she married Preston T. White and then she married me, see, and now I live in the Lower East Side with my cougar because my sister Trouble just moved to L.A. and ..."

He cut me off with a practiced "tell it to the hand" move, took a deep breath and sighed. He said, "Mister, you're 3,000 miles from L.A. I don't know what your troubles are, but you'll get a McDonald's burger at the station. Step over here, please."

I didn't get it. *Why doesn't anybody understand me?*

They were called New York's Finest for good reason. I'm sure it was to their complete and utter fascination that I continued my non-stop verbal situation report as they chauffeured me through intense holiday traffic across town until we arrived in their town car cop car.

The semi-noir dusk looked like my favorite time of year in Manhattan. Dazzling colored lights blinked and flashed their joyfulness, welcomed me with their sirens and bells. The blue people, men, elves, whatever they were, helped me out of the back seat of their sleigh. As they held the doors open for me to enter their enchanted workshop, I turned to the people behind us on the street and declared, "Merry Christmas to all! And to all, a good night!"

23

Mom

* * *

The stainless steel bench in the drunk tank chilled my butt through my whiskey-soaked pants. It was crowded, and I fit right in. The night's merrymakers weren't the kind that extended their pinky fingers when they imbibed.

Every brain cell in my head screamed with pain. I tried to think, tried to figure out where I was, why I was there, why I stunk so badly even the drunks avoided me. A guy in plainclothes stood by a uniformed cop as he swung open the door to the cage. "Wolfe!" he called. "You're out. You made bail."

In my mind, I stood up, strong and defiant, took determined strides to the door, rushed out of the cell. The reality was, I didn't make it. The men at the door picked me up off the floor and grumbled. They leaned over, grasped me under my arms, yanked me up on my feet. I remember being led and half-dragged to an empty gallery for the judge's arraignments. One of the men groused, "He's still drunk. He can't even stand up." They plunked me down into an aisle seat.

She stood before me with her arms akimbo. I thought, *Judges are getting prettier. But I don't like the way she's standing there, leaning forward with her hands on her hips. The expression on her face suggests my outcome does not look nearly as good as she does.*

Her distinguished facial features of prominent cheekbones and soft brown eyes, with a small dimple in her chin, cut through my blurred incomprehensive vision. I reached up; my clumsy fingers touched her thick, full hair. It was brownish, or reddish, or something. It cascaded past her shoulders and framed a face that was easy to admire. She wasn't in full focus, but I liked what I saw.

I said, "Hello, Judge. Come here often?"

She looked into my eyes and said, "Can you hear me? Sit up. What happened to you?"

I liked this one; I wanted to impress this one. It was time to turn on my smoothest *savoir faire*. I was obviously ahead in the game because she already seemed to know me. I didn't want to blow it and was careful to clearly enunciate, *"Why don't we go to your chambers and talk about it, if you know what I mean, and I think you do."*

She turned to my jailers. "What did he say?"

They exchanged quizzical looks. One said, "I think he said he likes you but, he's married?"

135

She said, "Officers, if it's all right with you, I'll have my bodyguards take him to our car."

"That's all right, ma'am," said one, "we have the capacity to do that." He pulled a handkerchief from his pocket and wiped his whiskey-stained hands. When he caught their stench he leaned over me, sniffed a couple of times. With an abrupt change of heart, he added, "We'll, we'll get your bodyguards. We can permit them to escort Mr. Wolfe outside."

When the uniformed cop walked away to beckon the judge's muscle, she entered her evidence against me. On a table before the high bench, the pretty lady spread the press proof of the *New York Daily Mirror* morning edition. I learned later that she made a call and obtained it from the publisher before its release.

I pulled up a chair, sat down and examined it. It was a big headline and it took me awhile to decipher its fuzzy two-inch letters. I stared at it, held it at arm's length as I studied it. I said to myself with a laugh, "Uh-oh. That poor guy. I bet he's in trouble!" The bold headline on the front page shouted:

DRUNK NICK WOLFE STANDS UP POTUS!

The shocking slap on my jaw stung my flesh and jarred my senses loose. It triggered an instant fight or flight reaction. My mind cleared; I had to fight, had to stay alive. I burst up, wrapped my arm around the plainclothesman's collar in a reverse headlock. I was a second away from snapping his neck when a strong, slender arm interceded and shielded him from my hold. I heard, "Nick! Stop! It's me! Don't fight us. We're the good guys!"

I recognized her voice. I could listen to the soft, full timbre of her contralto tonality all day and night. I stopped, relaxed my hold. The cop clutched his throat and gasped for air with deep, gulping breaths. I said, "Electra?"

She exhaled her relief. "Yes! Electra! Your wife. Little Nick's mother." She helped me sit. The other cop returned, accompanied by her twin towers of beef in their custom designer suits. They took their positions on each side of her like a pair of offensive guards.

She said, "I had to accept your Presidential Medal of Freedom on your behalf. The press is doing everything they can to humiliate John, not to mention you."

The plainclothes guy still coughed as he picked up the thin, yellow newsprint. He took a seat and examined it like he was reading the Sunday Funnies. His thinking came out loud. "Why would a guy get this way? He has the world on a string. And he gets staggering daylight drunk on Scotch."

Electra's head snapped to her side. She said, "Scotch? Nick hates Scotch."

The cop said, "Take a good whiff, ma'am. I just did. That's Scotch whiskey for sure. Good Scotch. Your husband had an expensive night on the town."

She leaned into me, nose to cheek. I felt her breath, marveled at her luscious cleavage, admired the tiny, nearly invisible downy hairs on her skin that caught the overhead lights. She sniffed my neck, took in a deep breath.

I closed my eyes and followed suit. Her body's delicious natural scent was enhanced with *Coco* by Chanel. I would have recognized her in a forest of tall trees on a moonless night. My lovely, wonderful wife; "Electra?"

When she stood up she said, "We need to backtrack him since we spoke yesterday afternoon. The first drunk Nick ever had as a teenager was Scotch with Coke. He thought he looked like a big shot and drank nine of them. The bartender wouldn't even mix them. It nauseates him to this day."

"I can vouch for that," said a voice I recognized. My wife introduced herself to the man who strode into the room in a trench coat. He said, "Lieutenant Moynihan, ma'am. Homicide."

She said, "Thank you for contacting us, Lieutenant. Was he involved in a homicide?"

"Not him directly," he said. "But I'm running the investigation of his friend's murder, and he constantly interferes with police business, mostly mine."

Electra said, "I'm not sure I understand."

"Ma'am, I gotta admit, your husband and I aren't what anybody would call friends. But as much as he gets in my way, I have to be honest. I know he doesn't touch Scotch.

"We met for a drink one night. It was Christmastime; the murder business was slow. They served him Chivas on the rocks by mistake. He blew it out the moment it touched his lips. The stuff makes him sick."

She said, "Then we need to find out why he's soaked in it."

Happy said, "Mrs. Wolfe, I don't like the way he does things. But I can't like the way he does things. I'm street legal. What he did rescuing all those kids in D.C. was great. And what you guys did down there at the Texas border is historic." He grimaced. "But ..." His voice trailed.

Electra finished his sentence for him when he paused. "But you wish he wasn't in your jurisdiction."

He grinned. "More or less. You two aren't moving down to your ranch in Texas by any chance, are you?" They shared a quiet laugh.

Electra's bodyguards towered over us like brothers of Goliath. I stumbled between *Saph* and *Lahmi* as they moved me outside and into the hotel's white limousine. They held the door open for Electra after they poured me into the back passenger compartment. She slid across the seat, sat beside me, laid her hand on my lap. I leaned against the window and stared outside at the passing storefronts as we rolled forward.

She turned and spoke to me in a voice made famous by Lucille Ball: "Nicky, you got a lot of 'splainin' to do."

24

Mom²

* * *

We sat in the penthouse of Electra's place of residence when she visited the Big Apple, the *Maison Blanche* hotel on Madison Avenue. As owner of the joint, she kept the luxurious two-floor penthouse reserved for her social visits to the city that never sleeps.

Every Christmas season, she flew the boys up in her blue Grumman Albatross and moored at the Skyports Seaplane Base on the East River. The Washingtonian family typically took in the lighting of the tree at Rockefeller Center, The Rockettes, Opera at The Met and in the past year, discovered my favorite two-star cuisine at the Metro Diner. On other occasions, her suites at Yankee stadium and the Meadowlands provided safe and comfortable settings when they followed their favorite teams in person.

That week, she brought the boys to celebrate the United States' 2026 sestercentennial throughout New York City. President Jackson was scheduled to speak to the nation from the base of the Statue of Liberty on Liberty Island. Fireworks galore would fill the sky along with the latest drone-created images. Like they did in the bicentennial celebrations of 1976, the Tall Ships would sail throughout New York Harbor and the Hudson River to honor the 250th anniversary of America. And the USA would party like it was 2026.

Cody the Cougar laid across my feet. The vibration of his purrs resonated through the snowy chenille of my hotel slippers. A hot shower and the comfort of fresh, clean clothes had given me an appetite. I leaned over and scratched the top of his head, asked him, "Hey, big guy. Where's room service?"

Electra quietly sat across from us in an overstuffed leather smoking chair, with an untouched morning cocktail nearby. Quiet, studious, patient. Mature. My wife could honeypot the Pope with her long auburn shag, those soft brown eyes, her refined features, and that drop-dead body. The spirit of love she transmitted from inside crossed between us and embraced me in a warm, welcoming hug. How could I not fall for this woman? And what was she thinking behind all that distracting beauty, anyway? "What the Hell happened?" I asked.

She said, "I was hoping you'd tell me. A lot of us are wondering that."

"Us?" It was early morning, and my recent exploits caused Mom to drink her breakfast. She took a demure sip from her Bloody Mary. Then, with fluid grace, she set it down on the cowhide coaster on her side table. The sexy south Texan shifted into Mom Mode when she spoke. Her comment was delivered with the deliberate sarcastic understatement of a mother who ran out of excuses for her delinquent son's mischief.

She said, "Oh, me, the president, the first lady, Governor Stinson, General Willoughby, Colonel Benjamin Royce, half of the TEXIAN motorcycle club, the world press, the boys ..." she let her summation drift. "And then Lieutenant Moynihan ..."

I said, "Happy was there?"

"That's what you're going to take away from all this? Happy Moynihan? Actually, it's a good thing he wasn't there. He's the one who called to get you bailed out of the precinct drunk tank."

I held my head in my hands. "Oh, God," I said.

My wife answered, "Nick, I don't think even He's going to get you out of this one. Tell me what happened after we talked on the phone."

* * *

There wasn't much to tell. The only verification of the four shots at my front door was a couple of chipped bricks and the third dimple in the armored *mallette*. Even that was obfuscated by the pair of pre-existing dents from what I figured were ballistics tests. There was no police record of the silenced rifle via the city's ShotSpotter drones.

I searched my memory and related every detail of what happened the previous night and day after we spoke on the phone. Monday night: opened the briefcase using Jack's cryptic 5.2.2.5., took Jet's phone call, fell asleep. Tuesday morning: booked Bellevue Restoration, stashed the briefcase guts in the hotel's safe deposit box, checked Cody into the penthouse, decoyed the empty case back at my place, had breakfast at the Metro, played Spy vs. Spy, then Jack's, Jet, Scoop, and Penn Station.

"What about Penn Station?"

"I went down the escalator, walked toward the All Trains exit."

"And?"

I said, "I hung around for a while." *Oh, come on. That was funny.* Whatever I was doing, it was not impressing my newlywed bride. The roll of her eyes and grimace on her face made it plain that I shouldn't pursue stand-up comedy.

"I got dumped on my head, waterboarded with whiskey while they interrogated me about Jack's briefcase. The next thing I knew I was looking at you. Wasn't I?"

"You kept calling me, 'Judge'."

I held my hands forward as if to be cuffed. I said, "OK. Take me to your chambers. Judge."

My high-spirited Texas ranch girlfriend took another taste of the lusty morning cocktail in her hand. Meanwhile, my elegant Washington society wife recapped in lucid detail. "So basically, you found Jack dead, talked to some people, beat up a guy in his home, disrupted the NYPD, took possession of Jack's evidence and have withheld said evidence. Then you got shot at and brought that ticking time bomb here before you were shanghaied, whiskey-boarded and dumped on our doorstep."

I said, "I was hanging upside down in an empty storage warehouse. Scrambled voices. That's all I remember."

"Do you remember guzzling Scotch?"

The thought made me feel nauseated. "They wanted to know what I knew. I was so drunk; I didn't know my name."

"So, you were shot at, then tortured, and you thought it was safe to stash Jack's box full of hazardous materials here? In my hotel–our hotel?"

"It gets better," I said. "I heard in the cab that Sol got killed."

"Sol?"

"The pawnbroker who had the attaché from Jack. That's who I got it from."

I wasn't crazy about the look she gave me. I said, "Baby, I brought it here before I went to the train station. Whoever is after me knows where I live and shot at me there. I couldn't leave it at home and go to D.C. Only I know that I'm here." I ran my hand down the long extent of the mountain lion's bottle-brush tail. "Besides you and Cody," I added.

She said, "Little Nick just loves him. We're going to be here, anyway. Your quandary brought us down a few days early."

I said, "I'm hungry."

"You ought to be," she said. "Your diet for 24 hours has been Scotch whiskey and concrete pavement."

Fifteen minutes later, the magic that is room service arrived. The bacon was thick, wide, peppered, and firmly charred but still chewy in the middle. It tasted salty, and sweet from overspill of the pancakes' Canadian pure maple syrup tapped at an 18th-century family farm in New Brunswick, Canada. Steam from the black Yuban coffee in my thick white ceramic cup entered my nose before it reached my lips. I leaned back into my chair and enjoyed the slow intake of a deep breath. As I exhaled, my mind provided color commentary: *Glorious.*

Why did we have to ruin it with our first major argument?

25

Oops!

* * *

E lectra said, "Now that you're sober you need to call Yvonne–immediately. She needs to know, John, President Jackson needs to, Hell, *everybody* needs to know what happened. Now that you're somewhat lucid."

I said in my caring, sharing, endearing way, "OK, Mom. Give me a minute. My strength is just coming back and these victuals are too good to get cold." Cody agreed. He liked bacon, too.

Her flushed look of consternation revealed a shade of defiance that was new to me. "Nick," she said, "whether you like it or not, you're global news. Right now, the world thinks you stood up the president for the highest award an American can receive–because you got drunk.

"If your Alamo defenders weren't all volunteers, you would have been considered as a Lieutenant Colonel for the Congressional Medal of Honor. And now social media videos everywhere show you stumbling around Manhattan, soused, that same day. This needs to be corrected in a big way, fast."

My room service breakfast still tasted good. Cody still agreed.

Electra's glass was empty. She held it up to the light, examined its dryness. A moment later she stirred a glass rod in a clear glass pitcher and poured herself an additional deep red spiked veggie smoothie. She poured one for my hair-of-the-dog, as well. She handed it to me and said, "We were fortunate Lieutenant Moynihan called Murgatroyd from his precinct. It might have taken days to find out what happened to you."

"Good old Happy," I said.

She sat and sank back into her plush chair. Her eyes softened and her body relaxed. Electra began with the slightest tinge of pride, added a dash of wit and stirred in a pinch of sarcasm. She said, "I come up to New York early for the celebrations and a nice family holiday weekend. Meanwhile, my husband is in the crossfire of two murders. You're carrying a briefcase full of something that somebody very high up with very large money will kill you to get. You've been shanghaied and tortured and dumped on the doorstep of my hotel. But nobody knows you're staying here, right?"

I let my newly clarified eyes drift along the lines of the beautiful woman who sat across from me. For the moment, I knew where her head was at more than she did. She was trying to determine whether she was confused, afraid, annoyed, or angry.

"Nick, what have you gotten yourself into this time? Is there a blonde bimbo in distress in there, too?"

"Nah," I said. "She's a brunette."

I watched Electra's emotional engine roar to life. She was about to zoom past Annoyed and floor it to Angry. *I'm not doing very well today; better talk fast.* "Natalie Cocks. You ran into her at Birknerhaus. Her Cocks TV empire is being pirated. I referred her case to Roscoe Ritter."

My wife wasn't used to Cody the house cougar, yet. She worked to ingratiate herself and make friends, but he was a guy's cat. I reached across from my chair to hers and handed her a strip of bacon. Her re-gifted donation brought a purring response of gratitude from the 153-pound *Felis Concolor*.

Electra's voice was a deep purr as well. I loved to listen when she spoke words that expressed her heart. We didn't do it often, but when we rode in a car, a taxi or a limo alone together, one of my favorite things to do was to simply lean back and let her gentle voice lick my ears like the dry velvet tongue of a doe.

"Can't we sit this one out?" she asked. "Aren't there eight other F.L.O.T.U.S. people out there?"

"Baby," I said, "I don't know what the Hell is going on out there. I don't know from presidential awards, or media hoopla, or rifle shots in the dark. But I do know one thing. Jack's killer is mine. And I'm not sitting that one out for anybody."

"You're forgetting about your partner," she said.

"Murgatroyd?" I asked. "He's strictly the inside man at our skunk works." Then, to score points, I added, "I talked to him about moving to D.C., by the way."

Her facial features tightened into a look I had not seen on her before. At that misplaced reply I was instantly jolted by the obnoxious alarm of my internal Blunder Buzzer. Mom was looking at me, and Mom was pissed. "Not *that* partner," she said. "*This* partner!"

Somewhere in far north Saskatchewan, a mountain man heard that bear trap slam shut around my ankle. I was nailed; I was poleaxed; I had nothing. I said, "Of course, baby. I meant on my cases."

"So did I!" she said.

Oops! I said, "Baby, I love you. I love being with you. If not for the pain of getting banged up in the first place, I'd stay at home for you to nurse me back to health every day. This is my business. Nick Wolfe, private investigator. And Nick Wolfe works alone."

I only had six weeks logged into the big book of married life and still had a lot to learn. With the grace of royalty, Electra rose from her chair. She leaned forward and softly kissed my forehead. In a calm and patient tone of voice reserved for those who rear children, she said, "I love you too, baby."

A few steps away, her slender fingers wrapped around her glass. She struck a standing position in the center of the room and faced me with her arms folded across her bounteous chest. Beyond that, I didn't notice much, other than the French tips on her fingernails; then, her bangs. French tips, bangs and auburn shag. French tips, bangs, long thick auburn shag and a 35-inch inseam. I looked straight ahead with the spellbound eyes of a boy who beheld his crush.

It was the first time I saw her arch one eyebrow that way. Class in Family Etiquette 101 was about to be conducted in the *Maison Blanche* penthouse. And I was its sole student. I took a long pull on my hair of the dog.

26

Family

* * *

"I'm thinking of the cases I've followed with you," she said. "You know, the ones you worked on alone." The tall, beautiful Texan finished the drink in her hand. She crossed over to the bar, replenished her spirits once again from the nearly empty pitcher. *I seem to have a knack for driving people to drink.*

"As I recall," she said, "you got yourself into a little predicament at the Birknerhaus Group on St. Thomas Island. *I* pulled your caboose out of that fire. Literally. And you almost got my Albatross shot up in the process. I would have made you pay for that."

I was launching every diversionary countermeasure I could. I came up with, "In the end, Yvonne would have paid you for it."

She plucked an ice cube from her highball glass, flicked it across the room at me. "Of course, all I did at the border was sacrifice my ranch's entire herd with 100,000 head from three counties.

Plus, my helicopter. On our honeymoon! You worked alone there–with a thousand other Alamo volunteers."

I recalled the sight of her chopper overhead in the bright sun of early morning, going down in flames. I thought, and fought to hold myself back from saying, *and you have no idea of the knot that twisted in my gut, the complete devastation I felt deep inside my heart when I watched you explode. The love of my life, destroyed, before my eyes, because you decided to help.*

I felt like I was sparring with Jet, caught in a corner and getting pummeled. I couldn't cover up enough; my only move was to fight my way out. I said, "If you were with me, it would get in the way. Not you. *It.* Having to worry about somebody else, anybody else. I'm too far gone to be a team guy anymore. Green Berets, Rangers, SEALs are team guys. They train as teams, live as teams, operate as teams.

"Even those guys–the best in the business–still have to get orders to deploy from JSOC. When you've got to get it done in a precision situation, you need somebody who's gone behind the fence. You get a D-Boy, Tier One. We don't wait on orders from JSOC. We don't wait on anybody. We just Go. Like I do with F.L.O.T.U.S. You couldn't keep up." I tuned the pitch of my next point to resonate with my bride from the Lone Star State. I proudly said, "You know, 'One Riot, One Ranger'."

Electra let her south Texas drawl escape when she said, "Nice trah, cowboy. Nicholas D. Wolfe, I'm so mad I could chew up nails and spit out a barbed wire fence!"

I told myself, *don't say it; don't say it. It's late in the game and you're down three touchdowns.* I threw my Hail Mary pass anyway. "You sure are pretty when you're mad." The words of my hackneyed compliment rolled off her like droplets of water from a duck's back.

She spoke in a stern tone. "Admit it. Somehow, somewhere, each time I have to pull you out from the point of no return. Like just now at the drunk tank. If I'm with you from the beginnings, the endings might not involve, 'the pain of getting banged up in the first place.'"

"And what would be the fun in that?" I asked. I never had a smile so underappreciated.

Electra's eyes said this was not the time for humor. Apparently her frustration had reached critical mass. She stood before Cody and me and let her gaze drift from my head to my toes, and from his tail to his nose, then back up to me again. I followed her eyes to the side of the room where Horace and Little Nick peeked at us around a corner for their ringside seats.

A slow, gradual reversal took place and spread across her face. I watched her features relax, then ease past the tension that strained them. Her body loosened. "And I'll probably have to save your cute little butt again with this one, whatever it is," she said. She stopped, relaxed a moment to reload. She looked down to hide the mist forming in her eyes. "What if I'm busy?"

Thank God, a break. "That's what I mean," I said. "You don't have time for this stuff. You have 650,000 acres of cattle ranch and an oil fracking company to run."

"Yes, it's a lot. And yes, I could use your help. Nick, it isn't the businesses I'm worried about." She stopped. She looked down into her glass, spoke without looking up. Her voice changed and lowered. It came out even softer and deeper. "This is the third time since I've known you that you've been captured, tortured and almost killed. I love you, Nick. I don't like being apart and I don't want to become a widow again. You have a family now; *we* have a family now."

The carbs, sugar, protein, and caffeine from my pancakes, maple syrup, bacon and coffee did their jobs. Chased by tastes of my Bloody Mary, they made me feel almost normal. I got up from my seat and walked to where she stood. She relaxed when I took her in my arms. For a while, we stood and held each other in silence. I said, "I don't want you around me when I have to be the way I have to be. Hell, I don't want to be around me when I have to be the way I have to be. But I have to be that way. Because I have to get the job done."

I felt the resonance of her soothing contralto voice in my chest when she said, "My big daddy papa bear. He can take on a dozen grizzlies by himself. But he's such a thoughtful guy. He doesn't want mama bear to be there for backup."

I said, "No, I don't. Papa bears are nice guys. Until somebody pisses us off. Then we get not nice. I don't want to be not nice around the woman I love."

She let out a soft chuckle and said, "I can decide that on my own, sir."

I spoke in a deep tone reserved for Truth, an attitude that emanated from within my chest and resonated in my throat like a slow verse in a Sinatra song. "We'll be fine, baby. But don't press me on this. I haven't received any Heavenly Directive on it like the others. There's some reason I'm out on this limb by myself, but it's something I have to do. For me. For Jack. I don't want you anywhere near the killing field. Then we can make bigger life plans."

I felt the rumbling resonance of our building before I heard the deep, distant explosion. The shockwave felt like a small earthquake and shook the hotel. Sirens sounded on the streets below. We stared at each other with blank faces and uncertain eyes.

27

Blast

* * *

Electra and I stood together, surrounded by cars, trucks and ambulances from FDNY and NYPD. Side by side, we held each other and stared into the blazing inferno two hundred feet away.

What had been my three-story warehouse on the lip of the East River crumbled before us, reduced to flaming, smoking, rubble. An inferno roared up through the roof. Bricks, mortar and steel collapsed; chunks of walls tumbled to the pavement below.

"Mommy," I said, "you'll do anything to get me to move to Washington."

She said, "I don't know how you can think this is funny! This is what I'm talking about, Nick! What if you and Cody were inside?"

When words fail, roll your own and light one up. I didn't roll my own, so I flamed on a Marlboro. I recalled a conversation I had with Jack in his office less than a year before. I was working on the case that took down the global pedophile cabal. Jack said, "Look, kid. If they want to take you out, they'll take you out. They'll blow your entire building down and kill 500 innocent people if they have to. They don't care!"

I needed to get as far as possible from anyone I cared about. In a tone of voice that did not permit discussion, Electra said, "You need to call Yvonne." I agreed, reached for my phone.

A dark stretch sedan with limo-black window tint pulled up a few feet away. An NYPD officer addressed the driver, then stepped around to the rear passenger door. When the opaque glass rolled down he spoke with the person in back. The driver got out and walked around the car to the door where the officer stood.

She was dressed in traditional chauffeur livery, but the way she filled it out was better than any teamster I ever saw. Her skin-tight ebony jodhpurs showed off legs that could step over women's high hurdles. A thick rope of dirty blonde hair was worn beneath her uniform's black cap in a French braid that stretched down between her shoulder blades. She was tall and looked out above most pedestrian masses with a front end as pronounced as a '57 Eldorado's rubber baby buggy bumpers.

She stood as a three-dimensional collaboration of black, white and gray fabric and leather that covered her alabastrine complexion. The only trace of color on her was a pair of dramatic 80s retro shades, intensely red with horizontal view slats. She turned in our direction, raised them with one finger. After she surveyed us and the surrounding area, she opened the rear passenger's door.

The vision that stepped from the Lincoln was a bombshell who made saxophones swoon, traffic stop, and men drive their cars into buildings. Avalon captivated the eyes of everyone on the block. A fireman on a boat on the East River manned a hose on the blazes that roared in my place. He turned to worship her with his eyes through a pair of binoculars; the nozzle followed, and he knocked a landlubber cop off his feet with its blast.

Her promenade to my position drew more attention than the catastrophic flames and wreckage at hand. Even the local news cameras diverted their attention to her. Avalon projected a vivid color contrast against the dark rubble and black smoke in a tight, bright yellow mini dress.

She paraded in matching canary heels as she made flirtatious finger waves to her adoring audience of first responders. Avalon greeted them all with a flashing smile and, "*Bonjour*, Boys!" A moment after she parked herself before me she made a quick sideways glance toward Electra. When the French beauty removed her Lamborghini shades and tossed her hair, I felt captivated by the power from her bewitching eyes. "Nick, darling! Are you all right? What happened?"

Avalon looked at Electra, then back at me. She said, "We drive from the Bowery Showroom in your Lower East Side. Ronaldo is such a diva. He needs me to appear. We heard the news in the car."

Amid the sounds of sirens, water hoses, bullhorns and flaming wreckage, I made stammering, clumsy introductions between my beautiful wife and the stunning fashion model. My failed attempt at gentlemanly diplomacy did little to dim the electricity that sparked in the air. I felt like I stood inside a Van de Graaff generator between two overcharged positive poles.

Avalon looked past us at the fiery wreckage from the blockwide blast. To break the awkward pause, I offered, "I seem to be having a fire sale on my place."

Electra elbowed my side. She adopted the same body posture of crossed arms I witnessed an hour before in our suite and asked Avalon, "How thoughtful of you to stop by. How did you know where Nick lives?"

Avalon gave an innocent smile. "*Pauvre petite garcon,*" she said. "Nicky was such a shining knight yesterday. He told me about it in the park; when he walked me home." She gave me a playful look. "He offered to sell me his quaint Bohemian *chateau.*"

Her face flirted back to me. Her index finger touched my chin; she looked into my eyes and spoke with a sympathetic tone in her accent. "Next time, you should come upstairs. You would see such beautiful views. Poor Nick. *Quelle dommage.* You do not want to leave New York, your sister moves away, your lion is lonely, your friend Jack is gone." She turned to Electra. "Such

160

a sweet man. He needs much encouragement at these times. *N'est pas?*"

Electra looked at me and said, "I can assure you. He'll get all the *n'est pas* he can handle."

The supermodel looked at my wife, then patted my chest. "He is such a dear man. I am so glad you are here to be with him (with her customary double ee's in *him*). Men need companionship during such adversities." She said, "*A bientot!*" and gave me a kiss on the cheek, then turned and walked away.

Did I say, walked? I don't know what it was. When Donna walked, she could lead a herd of men to leap off a cliff like lemmings. But this was different. With movements that transcended fashion, Avalon's steps went beyond any *haute couture* runway in Paris. The city street full of disaster and ruin turned into a pop-up one-woman New York fashion show.

As the *Vogue* icon receded, her image was a stark vision of human loveliness juxtaposed against the dark background of urban destruction. Her statuesque chauffeur waited by the rear door of the car. Avalon stopped before she stepped inside. "This is my *habitant*, Senta. You would have met Monday, if your cards were played the right way." She laughed. "*Au revoir!*"

Senta turned toward us, slid her red slotted shades down her nose with one finger. She made a quick glance at Electra, then gave me a blatant slow once-over. When she finished her head-to-toe inspections she stepped inside and drove away.

I carried a handkerchief in one pocket for just such unexpected emergencies and was able to wipe off most of Avalon's YSL *Rouge Pur Couture* lipstick. I didn't need to look to decipher Electra's mood; I felt it around me like a cold, wet blanket.

She turned back to the flaming, smoldering wreckage before us, said, "This is big trouble, Nick." She paused. "I understand that Bora Bora is nice this time of year."

I let out an indifferent laugh. Electra was not amused. "Nick, I know big money. Whoever did this has *fix-it* money. Your life means less than nothing to them and they can cover up anything. I want you out of this."

I said, "You sound like Jack."

"And Jack's dead! You're obviously too close to something too big, and these people won't stop until you're taken out."

"They'll stop," I said. "They'll stop because I'll have taken them out."

"Nick, I, I don't want this same thing to happen to our home with our family inside."

"It won't," I said. "If I'm not there."

"What does that mean?" she asked. "You weren't here, either!" Her eyes were wide open, wet, and getting wetter.

"Just until I get this thing behind me," I said. "Whatever it is, whoever it is, they won't be around to bother us when I'm finished with them."

She looked away, hiding her moistened eyes from mine. I held her arms and searched for her face until she reluctantly abandoned her visual evasion. Those honey-amber eyes beckoned, damming tears she did not want to release. Our kiss began softly, then increased its passion as our embrace grew stronger.

A moment later, I held her in a gentle bear hug and said, "Look, baby. If it's the last thing I do, I'm finding the son-of-a-bitch that killed Jack. We'll talk about everything. I promise. After I drive a stake through his heart."

Her face nestled into my shoulder. Without attempting a reply, she squeezed me. We stood together as the devastation of what had once been my home crumbled and crashed before us. I said, "I need to call Washington." I punched Yvonne Jackson's direct number into my phone and stuffed a finger into one ear. I had not been beaten up enough, yet.

28

POTUS

* * *

POTUS joined FLOTUS on our secured call. I tried to eavesdrop on the gears that turned inside his head, but that machinery was too well oiled for my pay grade. I didn't need the use of a voice-stress analyzer to detect that he was upset, but he was a statesman as well as a decision-maker.

The president asked three pinpoint questions:
"What happened?"
"How?"
"Why?"

Here we go again. I told him step by step the events of that day. My friend was killed. It looked like he was onto something big. I possessed whatever it was.

FLOTUS said, "Nick, you need to come in and debrief on this."

I said, "Jack's murder is important to me. I'm needed here, in the city."

President Jackson chimed in. "Wolfe, you might be involved in something more important than you know. You might not; but I'm not discussing it even over secured lines."

We each held our pause.

He added, "Somehow, every time you get your ass in a sling, you get mine involved along with it, but in the end you manage to turn cow patties into roses."

I said, "Thank you, sir."

"That isn't a compliment; it's an unfortunate fact. When The Boss tells you to get your ass down here, you get your ass down here. And she just told you to get your ass down here. So, get your ass down here."

Inside my head I twisted off like Daffy Duck: *I don't want to go to D.C.! I need to stay on my case! Staying hot on the trail of Jack's killer is my mission! She isn't my Boss! I don't have a Boss! They're probably just worried about national security ...* I paused my internal rant for a moment. *Listen to me: "They're probably just worried about national security." I sound deranged. Maybe I am.*

I answered, "Yes, sir."

29

F.L.O.T.U.S.

* * *

"Blah blah blah blah blah ..." *Politicians.* The next afternoon, President Jackson restrained his intense irritation behind the arm's length friendship we formed during my previous two adventures. The main reason he served as Best Man in our wedding was because his wife was my bride's best friend.

But John Jackson and my father had a close bond that went back to the president's childhood. My dad was in the French Foreign Legion in Djibouti and saved the future leader's young life when his school bus was kidnapped by pro-independence activists in 1976. Later, Dad became the Director of the DIA.

As I sat alone on the Oval Office couch and listened, it felt like I was nine years old and my father sat me down for a *talk*. Only the president's personal secret service detail and I heard him twist off. My Best Man read me the riot act from behind his historic Resolute Desk:

... He honored me before the entire world ... The President of the United States, in the White House Rose Garden ... I didn't show up ... A hundred people videoed me stumbling around drunk ... The globalist fake news media vilified both of us on TV, the internet, social media, radio and print ... Did I have any idea the amount of political capital it would take to overcome that? In an election year?

I know, I know; do I have to tell it again? I don't have time for this. There's a murderer waiting to meet the wrong end of my .45s. Why am I marking time in the White House?

In the training camps of my youth, I learned to keep my mouth shut and my ears open. I sat with well-feigned rapt attention. My rope-a-dope acquiescence survived several rounds of Chief Executive verbal pummeling.

After I related the order of events that took place Tuesday morning to his satisfaction, I departed the nation's *Sanctus Sanctorum.* Several of President Jackson's staffers shuffled in. They took their seats around the room to conduct other business.

A lovely brunette intern escorted me five stories down in an inconspicuous elevator's massive steel cage. At the bottom, a Sergeant of the White House Military Office walked beside me into the executive emergency bunker.

If you didn't like women with tall, lean, athletic figures and luscious Polynesian features, Yvonne Jackson wasn't your type.

If you didn't like dark almond eyes and silken black hair that draped down to the small of her back, she wouldn't have done it for you.

She did it for me.

We sat 3,500 feet below the north end of the White House in the 2010-era Deep Underground Command Center. The First Lady's secret service detail stood aside in the subterranean bunker she used as an office. Her pitch-black eyes unabashedly scrutinized me across her gray military-grade desk.

I scrutinized her back. Her *couture du jour* was a slimming dark business suit of charcoal gray Italian wool blend with a cream-colored silk blouse that draped on her like liquid fabric. Gorgeous, lucid, powerful, she was my kind of woman.

Yvonne Jackson supported the independent work of her personal team of civilian operators directly from the White House. F.L.O.T.U.S. ops kept the world safe for sanity and often got into precarious predicaments. When needed, FLOTUS exercised Executive Mansion clout and got us out of them.

The First Lady became a fan when I rescued little Nick. We connected on a personal mission of hers when I took down the congressional and overseas pedophile cabal with maximum prejudice. After that, she was astonished when she and all of Washington were wrong and I was right about the surprise attack immigration invasion across our southern border.

At Alamo II in Brackettville, Electra, Trouble, Josh Hitt and I joined with the Texas Army 3rd Brigade and the TEXIANS motorcycle club. We stood as 1,000 against a surprise invasion of 40,000 Chinese, Hamas and Cartel terrorists in the pre-dawn hours of Memorial Day. Yvonne Jackson loved my ass. I had the First Lady in the palm of my hand.

* * *

"Damn it, Nick!" she said. "You've gone too far! You may have been abducted; you may have been questioned; you may have been hazed; but your timing could not be worse."

Stunned, I thought, *What? "Hazed?" Wait a minute. I didn't have control over these people that shanghaied me. You didn't try to control me when I burned down the Birknerhaus Group and rescued a gaggle of kids; you didn't try to control me when I rounded up volunteers and saved the southern border. But now I have to drop what I'm doing, travel down here and mark time in the center of bureaucracy?* I said, "Yes ma'am."

"John is campaigning for November's national election; he's shot at twice and hit in the head once. The Secret Service fails him; the legal system wrongfully prosecutes him; the biased media pushes lies against him. And now, you–this! The President of the United States gets stood up on live television in front of the world, by a drunk!"

I edged some sleep out of one eye with a fingernail. I said, "Yes, ma'am."

"I wish you would move your business here to Washington. You wouldn't have been waylaid in Penn Station."

If wishes were horses, how we'd ride, ride, ride. I said, "Yes, ma'am."

"You really hate this, don't you?"

"Yes, ma'am."

"Will you please stop that?"

"Yes, ma' ..." I caught myself. "So, is this where I get my new, improved F.L.O.T.U.S. decoder ring?"

I thought her sense of humor was more lenient. I was wrong. "We need to talk about that," she said.

I made a deep inhalation and leaned back into my seat. *Yes, she's the First Lady. And, yes, she's hotter than a firecracker on the Fourth of July. And yes, I like her and yes, she's Electra's best friend. But this is exactly why I work alone. I don't need anybody in an ivory subterranean bunker telling me how to run my business. I'm on Jack's murder case. Period. What they do on their government time is up to them. I'm out of here.*

She observed my restlessness and in the process I read in her face that something was different. Thoughts played in her mind behind her obsidian eyes. "I've changed my mind," she said. "I think you're too close to the edge. You need a break. I want you to take a break. Spend more time with Electra and your family."

I said, "That sounds familiar." It was exactly what she told me before we defended the southern border from invasion on Memorial Day. I said, "That's exactly what you told me before we defended the southern border from invasion on Memorial Day."

She said, "Go home to New York, Nick. To your family in your hotel. Someone there needs to talk to you."

I said, "I know. Electra is on me big time to move things to D.C."

"This is someone else." Her eyes cut a nanosecond look toward her omnipresent protection. "But you need to talk to him there, not here."

I said, "Unless he's going to tell me who killed my friend Jack, he's going to have to take a number."

"It's about a murder. But this one hasn't happened yet."

The theme from the *The Twilight Zone* TV series twinkled in my brain.

Yvonne Jackson possessed great and deep intuition. She said, "Don't be that way. He came to us directly about an impending event. It is vital that we stop it. He thinks you have information that can help; that's all."

"That's all?" I asked. "And who's 'us'?"

"John, and I," she said. "Now, you."

She paused a moment. "He's waiting to meet with you," she said. "Don't worry. You'll be a normal citizen on the Fourth of July. You'll be with your family. But you may be able to help him with information you have." She waited, then repeated, "That's all."

"Is that an order?" I asked.

She leaned back in her chair behind her spartan desk, spoke in a sarcastic tone. "You know we don't give orders in F.L.O.T.U.S. You operate on your own. You do what you do. We, support you."

Of course you don't give orders. I was just chomping at the bit to return to the muck of The Swamp from my home in the Big Apple.

She read my mind. "Don't take this the wrong way," she said. "I choose the best of the best for F.L.O.T.U.S. And you are the best of those. But I've seen the self-imposed tragic circumstances that happen with your kind when you're too intense for too long. You need a break. I'm giving it to you whether you like it or not. I can't detain you from your murder case. But you're on temporary furlough from us for the time being."

I sensed the imminent arrival of another delaying request. Before she could think of an additional reason to take up my time, I said, "See you in St. Looey," and stood up from my chair. I made it to the open doorframe, gave a two fingered salute, said, "*Hasta Luego, senora.*"

She replied, "One more thing."

Arghhhhh! I held my turned body position so she could not read the exasperation on my face.

"We need you to address the media. It's the only way to hit the brakes on this thing. They're in the Press Briefing Room now. They're out of control slamming John–and you. One of the biggest days in our nation's history is just two days from now and we need to get this handled first. Today."

That told me the reason they wanted me in D.C. *Imagine that, politics.* She knew I hated the press. I told her they wouldn't believe me anyway, told her my only answers to questions would be "yes" or "no." So, here's how it went:

30

Press

*   *   *

The James S. Brady Press Briefing Room was smaller than I had imagined. The sea of unfriendly faces that I anticipated was only the size of a compressed Great Lake. But there was turbulent disrespect on the faces of the scribblers. Only a month after they anointed me a national hero, the White House press regarded me as a bum.

At the late afternoon briefing, Press Secretary Jess Blasdell introduced me. I went straight to the point. I didn't like them. They didn't like me. I didn't care.

I looked out at the rows of parasites seated before me and said, "I understand there's been a lot of fiction written about me lately. Here's the non-fiction. You want to know why I missed the president's award ceremony. I've been a little busy.

"Monday morning a friend of mine was murdered, stabbed in his back. That afternoon the cops stopped a guy behind me on the street with a rapier stuck down his pants, and not the romance novel kind, if you know what I mean, and I think you do." That one cracked their iron curtain. My ears picked up a couple of subdued chuckles.

I continued, "It gets better," I said. "A few hours later, I was shot at four times at my front door." Gasps. "Then, a funny thing happened to me on my way to Madison Square Garden. Tuesday afternoon, I entered Penn Station to come down here and receive the president's award. I woke up hanging upside down in a vacant space, interrogated, tortured, and whiskey-boarded before I was dumped from a car on Madison Avenue. That's where all your *newsreel footage* came from."

The gang of scribblers sat frozen in their seats. They didn't know what to do. They were White House Press Correspondents, not street reporters, and they were getting their story directly from the mud and the blood in the trenches. I saw that my timing was perfect; the shock and anxiety on their faces had strained to its peak.

"But wait, there's more!" I added. "Yesterday, my home in the Lower East Side was blown to Kingdom Come. Just flames, concrete rubble and twisted steel. Now, I'm here talking to you. So, what's up?"

I was peppered with asinine questions. The subjects ranged from what it felt like to watch my home burn, to what I thought of President Jackson's chances of winning the upcoming election, and did I like the First Lady's color of nail polish.

I played verbal Aikido with a couple of their gotcha questions by making quips and embellishing the truth whenever it made me look good. I picked up signals that the session turned in my favor. *I can play politics, too.*

When I wrapped up, I looked past the scribes into the cameras and said: "I don't know who is behind these events. I don't know if I care. What I do know is somebody murdered my friend."

I paused, listened to the whirr of their camera lenses rotating and zooming in tighter for dead-solid close-ups. When I spoke next, I looked the viewers at home directly in their eyes. "So, if you're the killer, take a good look. You know I'm coming after you, wherever you are. And you better hope the law beats me to you. Because you know I'm going to kill you, the same way you killed Jack."

There was no collective hush that fell over the chamber, no surprised silence among the reporters. The entire room gasped out loud—some jumped up from their seats and ran out as if in an old black and white courtroom drama.

Jess Blasdell rushed to the podium. He covered the mic with one hand and, with obvious discomfort, thanked me. I walked off stage toward the back room as he was peppered with questions from the screaming Fourth Estate.

FLOTUS glared at me. And then there was POTUS. The anger in the eyes of President John Jackson was restrained only by the public and media optics of the moment. He acted like he shook my hand and leaned in to speak into my ear. Beneath his practiced politician's underbreath, the president said, "What the Hell has gotten into you, Wolfe?"

Behind us, Jess announced that President Jackson would present my medal again at a later date. He followed that with the statement that all was understood and forgiven and I would be present on stage at the Statue of Liberty for the president's speech.

President Jackson smiled to the cameras and waved. He continued in an aside as he prepared to lead me backstage: "It's bad enough we have to perform a *Wag the Dog* distraction from your public drunkenness; now you're making vigilante death threats from the podium of the White House Press Room?"

"Look, I've got the briefcase."

POTUS looked at me and asked, "What are you talking about? What briefcase?"

"The briefcase I need to investigate. The one that's in New York. Where I was. Investigating it."

"What's in this briefcase?"

I said, "That's what I, and the people trying to kill me to get it, want to find out."

President Jackson looked aside at his wife, then back at me. He lowered the tone of his voice. "The Marine Nighthawk Squadron brought up one of their choppers from Anacostia. It's waiting for you outside. There's a plane ready at Andrews that will take you to New York."

I asked, "Why?"

"You need to get home," he said.

"With all due respect, sir, I only came to D.C. because you ..." I paused, looked at each of them. "But now you both want me to return to my smoking rubble?"

The features on his face tightened in an instinctive wince. The president said, "If you had any sense, you'd live here across the street, where you belong."

I said, "Mr. President, if I had any sense, I'd be fishing for tarpon in the Florida Keys." Then I added, "Electra brought the family to New York for your speech on Liberty Island Saturday. We're at the *Maison Blanche.*"

Yvonne said, "We are aware of that. I spoke with Electra on the phone. Things have come up since you and I talked yesterday. Someone else approached me. Privately. Individually. It's a matter of life and death."

She indicated her husband with a slight head tilt and eye shift. "His. If our man is correct, we don't trust anyone. The Deep State is too entrenched throughout the swamp. Based on the corruption we're uncovering after the last two attempts, we can't trust anybody."

I said, "A secret is only as good as the square of the people who know it."

President Jackson said, "That's why your colleague who came to me is the only one we're listening to."

"Sir," I said. "I've just been put on a F.L.O.T.U.S. furlough."

"True," he said. "This isn't to get yourself involved. He wants to examine what you have. This briefcase of yours may be more important than you think." He added under his breath, "I don't think we could handle the body count if we got you involved."

"I'm in," I said. I couldn't wait to get out of there. "Who's 'he?' If I'm sharing the contents of Jack's briefcase, I'd like to know who my dancing partner is."

A member of the White House office approached and handed the president a note from his Chief of Staff. He glanced at its contents, turned to leave. "I'll have him meet you at your hotel. Good luck, Wolfe," he said, and was gone.

31

Pivot

* * *

In the late summer dusk, a White Hawk helicopter idled its props as it waited on the grounds of the Executive Estate. As we flew above Washington, D.C. I observed our national shrines beneath us, bathed in serene white lights. All the way to Joint Base Andrews, I rode alone.

Night had draped its darkness over Andrews Air Force Base when the 1st Airlift Squadron rolled out a retired Gulfstream C-20G. The long-range, high-speed military conversion seated 26 and could accommodate skids of cargo. Above the dazzling electric energy along the eastern seaboard, I rode alone.

I called ahead and Murgatroyd enlisted the services of our friends at Impervious for my return. Valeriy Bubka met me on the tarmac at LaGuardia when I arrived at dawn's break. I rode in the back of an armored Range Rover Sentinel from the airport through the world's most exciting city, alone.

All night and into the morning sunrise, my solitary thoughts were my only companions as I traveled, lost in a trance of concentration. This puzzle had a thousand pieces. I held a handful of them, but none connected. A corner piece here, some border edge pieces there, but no guts, no heart.

Something wasn't right. I stepped outside myself and gave an honest examination of my tradecraft skills. I had to admit; they looked like an athlete that's out of shape due to lack of competition.

I remembered when I registered to qualify for the Unit; I got the Speech from my CO. His friendly message was, if you leave your Ranger Battalion, you better qualify because you aren't coming back here if you don't. But I had innate skills that ranked at the top of even the elite Delta Force.

Navigation skills and situational awareness were mission critical in the Unit. One slip and you were likely dead. On every test of abstract concepts and map reading I scored in the top 95th percentile. In every branch of the service that I served–Puking Buzzards, Army Rangers, the Unit–I tested out at the top of every class in observation and surveillance. And I mustered out, alive.

Yet I missed several telltales in the past couple of days. My act as the bear in a shooting gallery at home warned me that they were much too close. I was after Jack's murderer and they were after me, because I had whatever was in Jack's briefcase that they didn't want me to have.

*   *   *

Throughout the three-legged trip home, my mind reached and grabbed at a swirling nebulous of facts and data. I tried to snatch pieces from the maelstrom of people and events in my mind and stick them together. But my morning immersion into the physical scramble of life in the city interjected itself with a grounding effect.

The tall revolving doors of Electra's *Maison Blanche* hotel spun around me, dazzling in the bright morning daylight. My reflection in their mirrors revealed a face that was a day past shaving on a disheveled guy in need of fresh clothes. I passed through the rotating looking glass into a wonderland of high-energy pedestrian traffic, motion, noise, music. I emerged through a culture shockwave into the reality of civilian city living on the other side.

I needed a few moments for mental decompression. Within a few hours I had traveled from a setting of blood, flames, and crime in the streets, to the White House Oval Office and Press Briefing Room, above the shrines of the nation's capital and the lights of the eastern seaboard, to our luxurious hotel and my loving family. I stepped into the gift store and picked up a deck of Reds.

Within the space and time of my ride to the top floor I performed a quick change of my psychological attire. In the hotel's vintage express elevator, I slipped out of the veteran P.I.'s mind-set of a ripped up and whiskey-soaked trench coat and into the mental state of a family guy's comfortable slippers and robe in a soft armchair before a fireplace. Recent events may have beaten me down to a five as a detective, but I needed to be a ten as a husband and dad when I walked through those doors to see my new family.

The polished walnut entryway to the penthouse suite swung open as I arrived. My eldest new stepson Horace was attired as usual, in complete gentleman's gentleman daytime wear. I had yet to learn what bet he lost to little Nick that placed him in the position of servitude for two years.

With his white gloved hand, he presented a polished silver tray. At its center sat a solitary highly desired item: a Waterford tumbler brimming with good-morning orange juice. I raised it to my lips for a welcomed taste to begin my day. The tang of vodka in the screwdriver snapped my head back. Horace smiled. Then, my coincidental namesake rushed across the room. Little Nick squeezed me around the waist in a strong, lasting hug.

So, this is what it's like. This is nice; this feels comfortable, warm. I like it here. But this isn't me; this has never been me. Every time I get near this, it evaporates and vanishes because somebody dies. I need to be on the streets; Jack needs me on the streets.

Then, she emerged. I didn't know from where, and I didn't care. From the sofa, from the bedroom, from behind the bar; when I saw her, I barely remembered where I was.

Electra appeared, and everything else faded away. No crime, no guns, no fighting, no killing, no death. When I looked at her, my face relaxed, my shoulders dropped an inch and all I saw was a vision of beauty within a soft golden aura of love. Her auburn mane of a long shag with bangs acted as a soft focus frame that caressed her cover-girl face.

Her sly smile warned me that she was about to play me like a poker star with a marked deck. Head to toe, Electra wore my favorite ensemble: snug, blue denim. A ranch shirt's white pearl snaps clung together like stalactites to keep from bursting apart against the centrifugal pressure from her curvaceous body. Tight ranch jeans hugged her long slender legs, tucked inside a pair of hand-made white ostrich cowboy boots.

Welcome home, Nick. This is your life now. Not bad for a street level guy from the Lower East Side. My pair of good versus evil angels, the miniature guardian spirits on my shoulders that fought and scrapped when I made decisions, walked toward each other and met halfway. They smiled, shook hands, lit each other's cigars and toasted drinks from a bottle of Jim Beam.

Electra's loveliness was magnetic; each time I beheld her my vision was captivated to the extent that I had to purposefully avert my eyes from staring. And the boys adopted me without a hitch. Hell, I saved little Nick from the perverts in the tunnels beneath D.C. But it seemed to mean as much to him that I took him out for real-life Halloween trick-or-treat in a neighborhood, away from Washingtonian society parties. And

184

Horace; Horace was a self-taught, rapid-fire genius, mysterious and quiet. I also observed a subtextual wit and understood he liked to tickle the ivories.

Face it Nick, things change. She took your name. Your home on the East River was a spartan fortress; the White Mansion is bigger than, and across the street from the White House. You married into a position of responsibility to help run 650,000 acres of McDonald Ranch in south Texas, plus White Petroleum's fracking operations. It could be worse. Your hideout is the Maison Blanche five-star hotel on Madison Avenue.

She came across to me, a soft sensuous angel in western wear. Her arms wrapped around me in a gentle embrace and she kissed me with slow, enchanting passion that took me somewhere else in the dark void behind my closed eyes.

A voice from the side of the room said, "You did well for yourself, Wolfe."

32

Conclave

* * *

What I recognized more than the voice's tenor was its trajectory. With reluctance, I looked around behind my wife, and down. He was seated in one of a pair of hunter green Egg Chairs by Arne Jacobsen. The suit he wore was a single button job, black with narrow lapels; his shirt was stark white, his tie solid gold.

The diminutive fellow's legs draped over the edge of the seat where his feet hung suspended above the floor. Sitting or standing, his voice came to my ears from the same height. The 4' 2" boss of the NSA's Antiterrorism/Force Protection Division rattled the ice cubes in his tall, sweaty glass and smiled. His voice keyed open a door that led to deep and complex niches in my memory of battles in Afghanistan. More recently, we met 18 months earlier when I took down the pedophiles.

I said, "Sky Lo Lo! How's the midget wrestling business? Or is it dwarf tossing now? I want to be sure I'm politically correct. Don't tell me you're the president's source?"

His smile disappeared. He said, "I have an office at Titanpointe on Thomas Street. And you're up a creek, my friend."

The last time we met I took him four bushel baskets of his favorite delicacy: fresh Chesapeake Bay Blue Crabs. At the NSA headquarters inside their visitor-friendly area called, "the red corridor," I traded for an ampule of liquid scopolamine and became an overnight fan of its 95% truth serum effectiveness.

Mr. Allison said when he contacted POTUS directly, the president went into the wayback machine and vetted the little big man. POTUS found that 20 years ago, Mr. Allison and I worked together in Afghanistan. He was CIA and I was a Hardy Boy.

He told me when and where to go. He told me when and how to get out. I went in. I killed terrorists. I got out. Mr. Allison was quick, fast, and kept his mouth shut. Consequently, when he traded his 9mm for a computer, he rose through the ranks with little resistance.

The little guy sipped his drink and said with a mischievous grin, "You're lucky to be alive." Mr. Allison drank Diet Dr Pepper. Mr. Allison only drank Diet Dr Pepper. I wondered if he bathed in it.

I said, "You know that stuff will stunt your growth."

Electra cut in. "We have a sitting room; you two can take this in there, please?" With a subtle movement of her head and eyes she indicated the two boys. I studied the trio that was my new family. "Allison," I said, "I'm the luckiest man alive."

He slid down out of his chair and we adjourned to a small library chamber. We took our seats on a pair of facing gold jacquard armchairs. Horace refreshed our drinks. When our sitting room was clear, I asked, "So, why are we in this conclave?"

"To save the president from assassination," came the reply.

I felt the corners of my mouth tighten. During my sojourn from the nation's capital, I thought of several possible scenarios. That was one of the pictures that my mind formed, among the cyclone of swirling puzzle pieces. I said, "I was afraid you were going to say that."

He said, "Only President Jackson and Yvonne know about this and about our meeting. It's just you, and just me. When he vetted me he saw our connection. That's when he and Yvonne insisted you go down to D.C.

"This has come together fast. Several agencies have targets on you. We aren't certain which, but between the swamp creatures in all the alphabet soup agencies there's enough Title 50 action in that grab bag that we don't trust anybody."

"Pretty severe, don't you think?"

"So is killing the president," he snapped.

He paused and tasted his Diet Dr Pepper in its sweaty glass. "You think Mack the Knife behind you on Bowery street was a bodega burglar? I'd like to sell you some beachfront property to surf Idaho. The swamp is so deep and so wide we don't know for certain how it's going down. I have my ideas, but there's a tall hill to climb and we don't have time."

"We?" I said. "I'm on my own case. And, I'm on F.L.O.T.U.S. furlough."

He said, "Wolfe, face it. The president is a known quantity. They know where he'll be, when and how. You're an unknown factor and your uncertainty makes you dangerous. They don't know what you have, but whatever it is, they believe it's critical. They believe it enough to take you out by blowing your home to smithereens, take sniper shots at you and hijack you to torture it out of you."

He looked like he wanted to settle back into his seat and relax with a smoke. Except, Mr. Allison didn't smoke. But I did. So, I did. I reached into a pocket for the pack of Reds I bought in the hotel's lobby store. I tapped one end and ripped the pull tab around the top of the cellophane wrapper, slid one out, popped it between my lips and lit it up. A long slow puff suspended itself in the air before me.

He said, "The Amtrack Police got Yvonne's call from your GPS and banged on that storeroom door. When they busted in, it was empty."

I tried to blow one smoke ring through another one. Normally, I failed. That time I drilled a bullseye. "Like I said, I'm the luckiest man alive."

Without any expression on his face, he said, "Wolfe, at this moment, you're more of a target than the president." If anyone trustworthy in government had known about that, it would have been the NSA's Antiterrorism/Force Protection Division's Mr. Allison.

I asked, "How do you know about all this?"

"I know everything," he said. "It's my job."

"So, who's the hired gun?" I asked. "Who do I have to kill?"

He said, "I don't know."

33

M.O.-FO

* * *

I couldn't help the aversion of my eyes to one side. I took in a breath, closed my lips and exhaled through my nose. I said, with no lack of sarcasm, "That imbues me with confidence."

Mr. Allison said, "There are six components: What, When, Where, Why, Who and How. The Why is obvious, and I've narrowed down What, When and Where. I don't know How and I don't know Who."

"Whom," I said.

"Him," he replied.

"No, you don't know *whom*."

"That's what I said."

"You said, you don't know who. It's correct to say, you don't know whom."

"Shut up," he said. "Is that correct enough for you? You drive me crazy, Wolfe."

"And I'm all you've got?" I asked. "Lucky you."

He said, "Who would you go to?" He paused and let it sink in. "Excuse me: 'To *whom* would you go?' The Secret Service? After that fiasco in Pennsylvania? 'It was a sloped roof.' Give me a break. You can't go to the Army's MI Corps, NIA, or the Marine snipers. The military industrial complex books are getting cracked open. They don't like anyone peeking under their trillion dollar covers.

"The NSA processes 320 million calls, texts and emails every day. We tap into a million miles of cables worldwide. I know everything that's going on everywhere. And the only things I can nail down about this are the money men and their point of origin."

"That's usually enough," I said.

"Not in this case," he said. "Too big. Too late. And no matter what, Jackson isn't backing down. He's speaking tomorrow."

I asked, "And none of our agencies can handle it?"

"Name the one you have confidence in right now."

I waited a beat for comic timing, then offered, "The FBI?" The mention of the once-respected agency, mired in corruption and cover ups, brought us together in a sardonic laugh.

"Sure," he said. "What's their number again? 86–48? Wolfe, it's what we don't know about this guy that's scary. He's your equal. Frankly speaking, I think he's more. Likely CIA

Paramilitary gone rogue, best killers in the world. And he's after you."

I made sure to employ my most sarcastic voice. "I should be flattered with so much attention," I said. "I'm put on involuntary furlough from an outfit that doesn't exist. That way I'm free to decoy shooters from every secret squirrel agency plus the assassin from Hell. I'll call Brioni House to rush a suit over with a big red target on its back."

"I wouldn't put it exactly like that," he said. "It's more of a coincidental benefit. I've picked up cross talk through HQ. I believe there's a third plot to kill him. I believe whatever you have in your briefcase has something to do with it. That's what they're after. They don't care about you and they'll take you out to get it."

"They've already tried," I said. Then I asked, "Observations? Track record? M.O.? Do you have *any*thing?"

He looked me up and down from his seated position, said, "Observation? Cowboy. Track Record? Lucky to be alive. M.O.? How about blasting in like Biggus Dickus on steroids and meth, blowing the Hell out of everybody and everything, then sorting out the solutions among the ashes?"

"Don't knock it until you've tried it," I said. "I meant his."

Mr. Allison replied, "He isn't like you controlled psychopathic killers. Only hits top targets. We know he shot Constantin Papi in Athens, we believe he also got Gerard Clicquot in Paris, and last year in Milan, Charlene Koch. Perhaps you've heard of them."

Of course, I heard of them. Everybody heard about them. Three emerging nationalistic world leaders, all slain in the past three years.

But nobody had a clue as to the identity of the phantom in the night that took them out. The authorities only learned the *modus operandi* after each hit was successful. Allison said, "His M.O. is no M.O. I even talked to our friends across the river, the targeting analysts. They're the best at finding someone, but they have to know who they're looking for, first."

He took a calming taste of his DDP on the rocks. After he doodled on his glass' condensation with his finger, he set it on its coaster. Without looking up he said, "Every hit's unique. Whatever it takes. Always a national leader. Always disappears. It was a basic sniper shot on Papi at the Parthenon with a .338 Lapua. We calculated 900 meters. But the other two ..." His voice trailed off.

"He took out three bodyguards in Paris before he got to Clicquot. With his hands. Two broken necks, one skull impaled six times with a sewing needle, and Clicquot, garroted."

"And you have no idea who this guy is?" I asked. "The NSA? The National Counterterrorism Center? The CIA? SAD SOG? Mossad?"

"It's SAC SOG, now," he said.

"Whatever," I said. Then, "A sewing needle?"

"A long green one, in through one temple and out through the other. Wasn't pretty," he said. "We know Where and When. I'm certain we know the powers behind the curtain. If you stretch red yarn strings point-to-point on a global wall map they all lead to Switzerland. But that doesn't do us much good the day before it's going to happen. Besides, we'd play Hell proving anything.

"We all know the Why: Jackson's cabinet is uncovering billions of corrupt dollars that support the globalists. They're afraid he'll unearth their scams. The What is his assassination. The When is tomorrow, and the Where is at the Statue of Liberty, during America's biggest sestercentennial celebration when he speaks to the world."

I swallowed my next thought with the taste of my screwdriver. "We're taking the hotel's tour boat to Liberty Island with the kids," I said. "I'll sit a few feet from him."

Mr. Allison said, "So will the Secret Service. And everything is in place tomorrow to prevent this from happening."

"It sounds like everything is covered," I said.

"They had things covered for Clicquot, Koch and Papi, too. We're dealing with the president's life against the top hit man in the world. The swamp is so deep, we can't trust anybody.

Outside of Jackson and family, there's you, me and the fencepost, and that's one too many."

"So, what happens to the fencepost?" I asked.

"I'm afraid your friend Jack found that out the hard way," he said. "He was the fencepost, and now you possess what he posted."

"Jack had two passions: the gym, and busting government corruption and coverups. He had everything on JFK: the six shooters in Dealey Plaza, what guns they used, where each one fired from, and that five were silenced and only one fired the recorded shots. Talk about money men, he knew the final greenlight meeting took place at an East Dallas diner on Grand Avenue and who sat at the table."

"Jack's gone," he reminded me. "And so is your home."

34

Detroit

* * *

I said, "So nobody wants me involved, but you're telling me we've got less than 24 hours to find out who the assassin is and stop them." I was getting impatient and annoyed. *This is ridiculous. I'm losing time and traction on Jack's murderer. I want to save the president, but I'm one guy. Why does this drop on me alone? I'm looking in from the outside at a bunch of bureaucrats. How do I know what everyone else is up to besides what I know? How do I know I'm not getting set up for something? This could be anything.* I drummed my fingers on the arm of my chair. I thought *there's only one way to find out.*

"OK," I said. "Deal me in. But I do things my way."

He said, "Wolfe, I learned a long time ago, 'When you own the opera house, you put up with the *prima donnas*.' That's why you're F.L.O.T.U.S. At this point, nobody else could handle you."

"I'm staying on my case," I said. "But I'm not averse to coaching from the sidelines."

I finished my morning health drink, eyed the orange pulp at the bottom of the glass. "You guys look at things the wrong way. You work from the ground, up. Data. More data. Crime scene data. Forensic data. Bits and bytes and granular details. 'Unredacted primary source data,' I think you call it."

He said, "In civilized society, it's called building a case."

"And it takes forever. I work from the top down," I said. "I get results and I get them fast because I talk to the boss, Daddy Warbucks. When you cut off the head, you kill the serpent. The body and all its parts drop to the deck. The rest is details for you guys to sweep into your bins with what you call your 'unredacted primary source data.'"

As much as he could without being swallowed by his seat, Allison leaned back in the chair. He steepled his fingers. When he spoke, he was no longer a little guy whose feet didn't reach the ground. He was the second in command of an international intelligence operation who presided at an HQ order-of-battle meeting.

"First, this happens tomorrow. Second, it happens here. Third, the powers behind it are in Europe. Fourth, you're a great op, but it may be too big for you. These global money men are more devious than you can comprehend. Mind you, I work with the top intelligence experts in the business."

"Hey, that's fine. I've got a killer to catch. Sayonara, baby." I began to stand from my seat.

He didn't look up at me. "Above the life of the president? Wolfe, it may sound callous, but Jack won't get any deader. You can still go full-on Inigo Montoya if the police don't nab him, first. This is to prevent a Chief Executive murder from taking place. Tomorrow."

I said, "I don't understand."

"It's too late and we know too little. The best we can do is throw a monkey wrench into the gears of their machine."

I asked a rhetorical question. "Like what?"

"Like you," he said. "You're my monkey wrench."

"You keep flattering me," I said. "Just to be clear, these 'top intelligence experts' you mention; are they the same ones that told you JFK was shot by a lone gunman? That 9-11 was a random terrorist event? That Building Seven collapsed out of what—magnetic resonance? Are those the 52 'top intelligence experts' that fabricated the whole Russian Collusion hoax and signed a public letter saying the president was a Russian asset? I'm trying to remember."

I shouldn't have said that. Those were his people; I was insulting his professional community. *Tough; I can't help it if his people and his community are crooked little bitches.* I was edgy, said, "If you're going to guilt me into it, let's get to it. Name names. I can't let the trail get cold on Jack's killer. I've got places to go, things to do, and several people are waiting to be folded, spindled and mutilated."

I volunteered my top suspects out loud, ashed my cigarette in the tray: "Totalitarian Numero Uno, Allistair Sonos?"

He compressed his lips, shook his head.

"Totalitarian Numero Two-Oh, Klaus Muller?"

His head shook in another silent negative reply.

My mind reached for Numero Three-Oh, but it was too big to consider. "The Rothberg family?"

"Bigger."

I sat back, stunned. "The German billionaire that crashes the economies of entire nations by globally shorting their currencies, the elitist leader of the Global Economic Forum, the ancient European family worth trillions? Bigger than those?"

Mr. Allison moved his hand along the arm of the ornate jacquard fabric. "I liked the chairs in the other room better," he said. "We're talking about the world's most powerful and secretive financial institution." He paused, thought a moment.

"Remember the early James Bond movies?" he asked. "Who were the bad guys? Dr. No, Auric Goldfinger, Emilio Largo. You thought each one was the ultimate villain. But it turned out they were all lieutenants to the man at the top of SPECTRE. Blofeld. You just named three lieutenants."

I said, "OK. So, where's Waldo? Detroit?"

Allison's sudden laugh expectorated his DDP through his nose. He recomposed himself, handkerchief in hand, then said, "How much do you know about international finance and central banks?"

I volunteered, "The petrodollar makes the world go round?"

"Give the man a Kewpie doll," he said. "Tell me what you know about the Bank of Global Settlements."

I couldn't keep my mind from sparking and shooting off in multiple directions: Jack, Electra, home bombed to smoking rubble, POTUS, FLOTUS, torture, Allison, the press–*Scotch*. The blank look on my face revealed the extent of my knowledge on the subject. It sounded familiar. I said, "Sounds familiar."

Before I arrived, Electra personally escorted the contents of Jack's briefcase from the hotel safe up to the penthouse suite. Horace brought the collection of its contents into the room on a large silver serving tray. Without words, he set it on the coffee table between us, then left.

Mr. Allison looked at me, nodded toward the tray full of media. I said, "I only opened his briefcase to see what's inside. This is my first opportunity to inspect this stuff."

35

Clues

* * *

Mr. Allison was one of the latent cryptographic geniuses the NSA recruited in the nineties from colleges. To him, three-dimensional chess was Pong. We examined each printed copy of hacked, cryptic emails, every thumb drive, every CD, and each document and map. We passed the deciphered documents back and forth and examined each one in close detail.

All leads added up to what Scoop told me. Jack's work laid out an exhaustive study of assassination plans, based on the hacked communications between global elite totalitarians. He detailed When and he showed Where.

They planned the hit for the greatest possible national detriment and global shock impact. All leads pointed to it happening on America's 250th birthday. The perfect setting would be during the president's speech from the base of the Statue of Liberty on the Fourth of July.

The big unsolved question was, How? Mr. Allison studied my former sensei's plans with detailed analyses of each lethal possibility. Jack had analyzed every imaginable manner of assassination, with near-clinical forensic detail.

Sniper Shots:

The closest straight-line distances to the Statue of Liberty were from Port Jersey, the Greenville Yards and Black Tom Island on the New Jersey side. They each provided workable shooting angles and distances if the president faced southeast out to sea along with Miss Liberty, to address the world. But President Jackson regarded this historic speech as a message to the American people on their birthday. He insisted that he faced northeast, toward the Battery, New York City, and America.

In that case, the three closest shooting points were all on the wrong side of 27,000 tons of the monument's massive concrete pedestal. An accurate shot from any of them was impossible. And a different location didn't fare any better. The straight-line range to Liberty Island from the Battery, on the southwest edge of Lower Manhattan was nearly 3,000 yards.

The distance from Castle Williams on Governor's Island to Liberty Island was workable, 1,400 yards across the Hudson. The former fortress was abandoned and empty and provided plenty of open windows with clear views of the Statue. But on that particular Fourth, the small island tourist destination would be covered with thousands of onlookers as a prime

203

viewpoint of Lady Liberty and the boats on the Hudson. The entire island would be standing room only.

Ellis Island offered the closest possible shooting site, three quarters of a mile from the Statue. The sniper range from its southern corner was possible, but it would have taken one helluva shot. A hit would have required the travel of a rifle's projectile over 1,300 yards of the Hudson River. The bullet would have to fight through ocean winds strong enough to push large boats around. And many of those "Tall Ships" had tall masts. That thick forest of high timbers with huge, unfurled sails and stars and stripes flags would present a supreme challenge of unpredictable moving obstructions to a sniper.

None of those distances was impossible. I've seen ELM shooting competition teams hit five out of five shots over 3,500 yards. Maximum shooting capability at that range would have involved a .50 caliber Barrett heavy sniper rifle. At 1,500 yards, the energy of the 660-grain bullet would drop 84 percent from 13,000 foot pounds down to 2,100. That would still be 600 foot pounds greater than the most powerful .44 magnum.

Mr. Allison said, "But let's say they get an AR-50 to fire that aircraft cartridge. Let's give them every break and say that they make their shot. That's thirteen hundred yards with a hang time of two and a half seconds. Over that travel time the bullet goes through the winds, across open seawater, between the randomly moving masts and sails of hundreds of tall ships, among hundreds of other boats. But let's say they cut through all that with no deflection and score a hit on target."

With a small sigh he said, "That great shot by that big gun that overcame all those challenges and obstructions would be rendered ineffective. He's protected at the stage by A-12 level multi-layered ballistic glass. It stops a .50 cal dead at 50 yards, as damaged as a windshield from a fat bug."

As we studied Jack's maps, ballistics, and trajectories, I asked, "Won't the Secret Service have scoped out these locations in advance?"

The only image missing from the look he gave me was a pair of Pince Nez glasses halfway down his nose. "Perimeter security? In Pennsylvania, they couldn't spot a sniper in dark clothes on top of a wide open white roof 140 yards away. It was the number one prime sniper location and they didn't even put anyone up there. Based on everything that's happened lately, do you trust anybody with this?"

We pressed on.

Air Attack:

With snipers ruled out, Jack examined every possible threat by air. The Blackhawk helicopters and F-35s scheduled to patrol the area before, during, and after the event solved that problem. That day, the airspace was closed down to civilian traffic and orbiting satellites were scheduled to record and relay close-up detailed videos of the area.

Water Assault:

The only other possibilities were surface and underwater boats. The air cover would aid surface security with its skyborne surveillance. Among the hundreds of floating party barges, the Coast Guard, Navy, Marines and New York Harbor Police shared patrol duties. There would be overt and covert craft, above the surface and below as well.

Statue Security:

Bomb-sniffing dogs worked a constant vigil throughout Liberty Island and within Lady Liberty for 24 hours before and during the event. The patrol teams were paired from cross-jurisdictional departments to reduce the chance of sabotage.

Every alternative assassination scenario failed. Jack's conclusion after his intense, exhaustive examination of every lethal possibility for How was basically: "Hell, I don't know."

But he had the goods on the financial backers of the two recent murder attempts. His overseas exiled hacker friends sent him paper trails of emails and bank transfers. Jack connected the dots of complicated money-laundering transfers from one shell corporation to another. He was convinced the same group was behind this forthcoming attempt as well. Allison agreed.

I didn't like it. I wished POTUS would have employed the use of a body double.

After several hours of deliberation, I said, "So what do we do? According to Jack, and according to you, at one of the nation's most historic events, we know a major hit's going down and we can only watch the fireworks and eat popcorn."

He asked, "Got another DDP?" A minute later, Horace returned with a glass of the stuff, on the rocks. Allison said, "We have everything else, but we still don't know How and we don't know Who-*m*. The only way you can cut the head off the serpent in time to put the kibosh on it is to hitch a ride on an SR-71 Blackbird to Switzerland."

"Why? Who? Where?"

"You think global power is divided between nations? I forgot, you're a big secret society guy."

"I torched the Birknerhaus Group," I growled. "That's as big as it gets."

He paused. "Let's get real," he said. "We aren't talking about the Royal Antediluvian Order of Buffaloes. Jack told us who's behind it right here. It's in these hacked emails, and I concur. Every two years, the CEOs of the central banks of 62 nations meet in Switzerland at the Bank of Global Settlements. And there is one CEO over the other 62, the central bank CEO over the world's central bank CEOs. If you want to follow the money, he's the leprechaun at the end of the rainbow."

"Blofeld?" I asked.

"This guy makes Ernst Stavro Blofeld look like an acolyte, but in the real world. This is the man that orchestrates the funding of every operation worldwide that tries to take down the United States. He funnels cash through his lieutenants at the BGS round table into their sympathetic nations' central banks. At least, that's my best guess."

"I didn't know you ever guessed."

"I don't," he said. "His name is Rudolf Keitel. If you want to cut the head off the serpent, he's the Black Mamba."

"Rudolf Keitel?" I asked. "You're joking." I couldn't help but smile. "Rudolf Keitel?"

"I fail to see how you find this amusing, Wolfe."

If I held a beer I would have handed it to him. I said, "Give me a second." I slid my smartphone from my jacket pocket, quickly touched a stored number in my Contacts. Fortunately, he picked up on the other end.

36

Rudy

* * *

"**R**oscoe. Nick. Where are you?"

"Downstairs," he said. "Where are you?"

The incredulous tone of my voice registered my disbelief. "Downstairs? In the hotel?"

"In my office. What hotel?"

"I thought you were in Schutzenmattpark, Switzerland. How are you here in New York? Did you ever leave on Natalie's case?"

He said, "The magic of private jet travel at 500 miles an hour there and back, my boy. And you are about to be $40,000,000 richer."

I thought a moment, then asked, "Roscoe, what are you drinking? Are you at the racetrack?"

His reply came back with genuine surprise. "What are you talking about? My jet lag hasn't caught up with me, yet, but,"

I cut him off. I was going to be upset if he blew the case I handed him on a silver platter. "Did she dump you after you left my office? Roscoe, I brought you into that case."

"You brought me in," he said, "and I delivered, *mein herr*. Case Closed. As in C-L-O-S ... You know the rest. Hell, I had most of it figured out and documented by the time we touched down at the airport in France. The BGS found in favor of Our Miss Cocks."

I was speechless. Before I was able to offer my startled congratulations, he conversationally stuffed me with, "To the tune of a one-billion-dollar settlement, thank you very much."

My only reply was stunned silence. Whatever he said next must have stuck in my deep internal memory bank, because somehow I recalled all of it, but I was so shocked at the time I didn't remember hearing a word he said.

His speech was matter of fact. "She called him. We walked in. He was there. All his cronies were there. We presented our evidence. It was the best timing, the best set of circumstances, the best assemblage of pissed-off people. Somebody up there likes me and I can tell you with certainty they all hate *Produzioni Unicorno*. That's the culprit–the company doing the pirate streaming of her programs. *Produzioni Unicorno*."

He made a clicking sound with his mouth, then said: "And you get four percent, remember?"

I was too busy processing what I was hearing. *This is Roscoe. I know Roscoe. He doesn't do drugs and he doesn't sound drunk. Roscoe wouldn't make this up. He just solved a case on my behalf that I threw away. And he's telling me it's the single biggest payday of my life. A billion dollar settlement, at the headquarters of the Bank of Global Settlements in Switzerland. Roscoe has a random access memory that borders on limitless depth and mystery, but this is mind-boggling news. I need to check this out in person.*

I said, "We can haggle about it when I get back from there, myself."

"Why are you going over there?" he asked.

"To see Rudolf Keitel, the same guy you did, but I can't tell you why."

"Why?"

"I can't tell you."

"I mean, why are you going to Switzerland to see him?"

"Roscoe, don't be an idiot." I paused, then said, "Meet me in my office in half an hour. I'm grabbing my gear before we head out." Click.

I gave Electra a quick hug as I hurried to the door with Mr. Allison and said with a wink, "Fire up the jet, baby. The president needs me to fly to Schutzenmattpark, Switzerland. I'll explain on the way."

The only words I heard on my way out the door were from Little Nick. "Can I go? I want to go!"

37

Otis

* * *

The dedicated penthouse suite elevator was the original Otis antique from when the landmark hotel was built in the forties. After the scissored accordion gate pulled across before us, the door clicked shut and we began our express descent to the lobby.

I watched the white graffiti paint on the walls of the elevator shaft pass by during our descent. "If I'm successful," I said, "if I get to this guy and cancel the hit, you're going to have to vouch for me. They won't know anything about something that doesn't happen. It'll be the second time in a week I've stood up the president."

Mr. Allison looked up at me and said, "That's your M.O. They'll recognize it." He smiled. Then he added, "I would suggest more thorough preparation than your usual cavalier attitude toward things. It doesn't get any bigger than this."

"I've taken down totalitarians," I growled.

"You're not 'taking down totalitarians,'" he said in a mocking imitation of my voice. "You're cutting off the head of the global conspiracy in our last-ditch, last-minute effort to prevent the assassination of the President."

I yawned and looked at my watch. For an entire two seconds I admired the soft gold beauty of the Rolex "Eye of the Tiger" given to me by the girlfriend of an Afghan warlord. *It's a long story.* I said, "Here's what'll happen. It'll take eight hours to jet over there. Another eight hours to sneak around, break in, take out a bunch of bodyguards. Then just in time, before noon, New York time, I'll put the snatch on some old bald Nazi and end up torturing him while he slobbers until he talks. Hopefully he'll call off the hit before I may or may not drop him from an Alpine gondola. Not exactly my idea of hot dogs and fireworks with the wife and kids on the Fourth of July. Plus, I'm on F.L.O.T.U.S. furlough."

Mr. Allison reached inside the breast pocket of his dark suit. He temporarily transformed into his alter ego, Dr. Feelgood, and held out a small glass ampule of clear serum. "And here is your precious scopolamine," he said without a smile.

Scopolamine: also known as hyoscine, *levo*-duboisine and *burundanga;* the world's most effective *veritas elixir.* It was prescribed in other forms for abdominal cramps or motion sickness. But it's clear liquid, injected into the base of the spine, made even the most hardened criminals tell the truth with 95% accuracy. I held the tiny vessel up to the light. It's colorless, odorless and tasteless contents turned amber before our elevator cabin's Art Deco sconce. I dropped it into my pocket.

He added, "You know, that stuff isn't easy to get. Even for me. I had to convince the guys over at the Mission Support Squadron in ISA that your wife was having an affair."

Before I could react and wring his neck, he exclaimed, "Kidding! Kidding!"

There was no music in the antique metal cage, only the sound of an occasional scrape against a wall. I looked out at the passing doors and floors. Beneath my breath, I mocked the tones of a Midwest American housewife and husband: "It's the biggest Fourth of July in 50 years. The Statue of Liberty. With the president. We'll take the boat with the boys. It'll be great!" Then I mocked myself. "Sorry honey, can't do it; gotta interrogate the Aryan superior race."

In a *non-sequitur* departure from any conversation I ever had with the man, Mr. Allison said, "Nick, from what I've seen upstairs, I need to say something. Are you aware of the divorce rate among special forces ops?"

I thought, *Nick? He never called me by my first name; not once in 21 years.* Of course, I knew. I said, "About the same as the old MAC SOG casualty rate. A hundred percent."

"That makes sense," he said. "Based on that historical data, you have a 100 percent chance of getting both shot up and divorced, or in your case, you can move into a mansion with your new family, private jet and billions. That's a beautiful woman I met back there, and some pretty cool kids."

The atmosphere in our descending metal box grew reticent. An echo inside the recesses of my head repeated everything I just heard as we lowered toward the lobby. I said, "You know what you can do with your historical data."

"Nick, I've seen what happens to some of your guys after a while, when it all comes back and hits them too hard for too long. They stand on bridges at midnight before they decide to jump. You have a rare opportunity. If you walk away now, you can cash out and own the casino."

"Now? You just browbeat me into this. I'm already in the middle of my own case, just referred another big one to a colleague, and you're dropping the fate of the world on me with this thing."

"After now," he said. "You're the luckiest man in the world. You'll figure it out." Before we got to the bottom he added, "*Buona Fortuna*, Wolfe. Be sure I get my Blue Crabs." When we stepped out into the lobby, we no longer knew each other and went our separate ways.

I had to admit, the *Maison Blanche* was a swanky joint: white marble floors and columns, uniformed doormen and bell hops in white with gold piping and shoulder braids, gorgeous ladies throughout, first rate bar and an award-winning five-star restaurant.

I heard, "Hello, Mr. Wolfe," here, "Good afternoon, Mr. Wolfe," there, "Nice to see you, Mr. Wolfe," everywhere. *Never knew I was so popular. Feels nice.*

38

$90,000,000

* * *

The driver of my hack couldn't have beaten Gimpy McLimpy in a quarter mile if he had a furlong head start. Twenty blocks took 25 minutes. I jumped out at the base of my building.

In most New York city offices, the front desks offered a *Cosmopolitan*, *New York* or *Grub Street* magazine. Not mine. Donna closed her issue of *Shooting Times* as she looked up. With the prestidigitation of a magician, she shoved something into a desk drawer. "Roscoe's on his way up," she said.

The rest of the office was quiet. "Good," I said. "What's that?"

"Oh, nothing," she said. Her mood was different than usual, not smiling, not happy.

I tried to put on a grin for her. "Looked like a .38 caliber nothing to me."

"I've been practicing," she said.

I changed my voice into mock-film-noir mode: "Make with the gat, doll."

She produced the handgun from her drawer, handed it to me butt first. I observed it out loud. "Smith and Wesson, snub-nosed hammerless .38 with rubber grips," I said. "Same as mine. Nice work."

"I learn from the best," she said. "I got my permit last week."

Both of our glass French doors pushed open. The large guy who floated through seemed to have gained weight since the last time I saw him only four days before. His previous butterscotch pinstripe suit had been exchanged for a massive dark purple single button affair; perfect for *Clue's* Professor Plum. I said, "Hey, you look like Professor Plum."

"Don't knock the threads" he said. "When I meet with people, they don't forget who was there."

I said, "Come into my office while I throw some things together." I grabbed a black ballistic fabric bag I kept stashed in a credenza cabinet. He followed me in and I said, "I can't believe you've been there and back and, really? Got the deal done?"

"The settlement was a billion bucks, baby. So now, Natalie wants to have *my* baby. We get a cool $90,000,000 payday. Better than cash. Gold Swiss francs. And I can use my cut."

I couldn't help the tone of frustration in my voice. "Don't lose it at the track, Roscoe."

He said, "Hell, Nick. I can buy the track now."

"We can haggle over your cut later," I said. "How do I get to Rudolf Keitel?"

"Rudy?" he asked. "You need an introduction to Rudy? That's an aftermarket add-on service. It might require the one percent in question regarding my share."

"We'll talk," I said. "How do I get to ..."

Roscoe called out to Donna through my open office door. "Hey, beautiful? Bring me a coffee and Danish?" He winked at me, added, "I promise I'll make it worth your while."

I grimaced and walked from behind my desk to my office entrance. I stood in the doorframe between the two of them, said to Donna, "Hey, gorgeous. Lay that pistol down. He knows not what he says."

Her promenade across to me with the requested fare was not her usual Donna Walk. She had tucked her snub-nose into a black waistband holster. And I was glad I wasn't Roscoe when she said, "He damn well does." When she returned to her desk she replaced her issue of *Shooting Times* with the last printed issue of *Soldier of Fortune*. "I think I'll read the classifieds," she said. "Some hit men might be out of work."

I smiled when I handed Roscoe his snack. "You're treading on thin ice, buddy. And you've gained weight."

He scoffed. "Ah, she loves me."

I said, "You're delusional."

He smiled like a man who held a royal flush in a hand of five-card stud. "And you need to party with Rudy Keitel, with no notice."

As I stuffed some stuff into my gear bag I said, "I asked Electra to fire up her Gulfstream for us. I'm sure you'll find her plane's catering superior to Natalie's. Tell me how we get to Keitel."

He took a bite from his Danish and washed it down with a gulp of coffee. "I'm not going back to Switzerland," he said.

"Roscoe, this is big, as big as it gets. And it's imminent. He holds the key to me shutting it down. I need you to go."

"I'm not going," he said, "because he isn't there." He paused, tasted his coffee. "I know where he is. But if I'm in on this thing with you, I need to know what's going on."

"You're not 'in on this thing!'" I said. "You don't have a *need to know* on this."

Roscoe stopped. "Oh," he said. "It's like that." He calmly sipped his coffee, took a delicate bite from his pastry. As if at high tea with Emily Post, he raised one eyebrow and extended his pinky finger from the handle of his cup. My office window's view over the East River occupied his earnest attention as he hummed a quiet tune. Time passed.

39

Teeth

* * *

I watched; I listened; I waited. So did he. I wanted to wring his neck but I couldn't hang him outside my 23rd story window. I told him what was going on.

He said, "Why didn't you say so? Rudy and I are old drinking buddies now. I had the deal almost done Tuesday night, wrapped it up Wednesday and we partied all night, wait, is Friday today? Yeah, Wednesday into yesterday. He got excited about the bet Malcom Rothberg welched on. Hates the guy. Rudy's embarrassing him through his family, just to piss him off."

"Roscoe, time is of the essence. Where do I get to him? Now!"

"Here," he said. "I mean, he's here, in New York." He took another bite. A piece of pastry dangled from the corner of his mouth. "We flew back with signed papers from him yesterday. He's in town today and he's here for the weekend, through Monday."

The weight of my half-full gear bag strained at its handle in my hands. I stopped, set it down on the floor, took my seat behind my desk, confounded. With one open hand, I calmly indicated for Roscoe to do the same in a side chair. After a pregnant pause that extended into its second term, I asked, "What?"

He said, "Rudolf Keitel. He's here, in New York City. We almost flew back together."

Still confused, I asked with deliberate tenderness out of suspicion that what I was about to hear was something I did not want to hear. "Why?"

Roscoe chuckled to himself as if he was in the know with an inside joke. "That's right," he said. "You've never seen him. Bad teeth! Hell, Nick they all have bad teeth. You'd think in Switzerland, but ..." He winced. "Yikes!"

I couldn't help the incredulous tone of my disbelief. "The CEO of the Bank of Global Settlements, in Switzerland, flies to New York for dental work?"

"Hey," he said, "they may be medical whiz kids over there, but they don't know beans about teeth. He needs a full-mouth reconstruction. The world's foremost guy for full-mouth work and occlusion is here. Started working on his smile design yesterday."

As well as this was going, I had to ask, "Here? As in our building?"

He laughed. "This building? In this neighborhood? We're talking about Dr. Anderson Jorgenson. Professor Emeritus at the Dawson Academy in Florida. Dentists pay $40,000 for one weekend to learn a single procedure from him. Dude, he's on Park Avenue."

"The top cosmetic dentist in the world is seeing a patient, on Friday, July 3rd?"

He said, "Money talks, Bubba. He tied his dental work into the trip, cut a deal with the doc. A big deal, as I understand. Rudy made special plans to be here for our big festivities tomorrow."

I thought, *I know why he wants to be here for the big festivities. For an event of this magnitude he wants to make sure his investment is secure, in person. What other things has he overseen while visiting our fair city? Who shot at me? Who shanghaied me? Who blew my home to Hell?*

I said, "Let's get out of here." Roscoe rumbled along behind me as I passed Donna's desk. I stopped when it hit me that she was in the office, working. "Donna, this is Friday, the 3rd of July. What are you doing here? Take the day off. *Yeeesh!*" I had a few things on my mind.

"Thanks," she said. "It's all right, doesn't matter."

"OK," I said. "Have fun over the weekend ..." I caught myself. *Wait a minute. Something isn't right.* "What do you mean, 'it doesn't matter'?"

"Oh," she said with a deep exhale. "Louis."

I stopped my momentum out the door. I wasn't physically moving that direction yet, but I stopped my mental momentum with what I was thinking. "Oh, no," I said. "I'm sorry, Donna."

She was a tough Bed-Stuy, do-or-die girl; there was no way she was going to let anyone see her emotional response to getting dumped by her boyfriend on the Fourth of July weekend. "Where are you going?" she asked.

"Dentist's office," I said.

She wiped one eye with a quick knuckle and rustled through her calendar.

"It isn't in there," I said. "This is an impromptu visit."

She sat back in her seat, frustrated, and not for the lack of recording my non-scheduled dentist's meeting. Behind my back, I jerked Roscoe's sleeve with a subtle tug. He stopped.

I asked, "Donna, do you have plans for tomorrow?"

"Not anymore," she said.

"Mine have made a quick change, too. Come with us on the hotel's launch with the kids. You'll get to sit on stage with the president when he speaks. Call Electra so you're cleared in advance. Tell her that that Switzerland is off and I'll talk to her later. Right now, I've got to move."

Her face shone its natural Italian beauty when she smiled. "Really? That would be great, Nick. I'll call her. Thanks. 'Switzerland is off.'"

I turned to Roscoe as we pushed out through our office doors. "How do you know so much about cosmetic dentistry?" I asked.

He flashed a billboard-sized smile with his set of oversized chompers. "If anybody knows teeth," he said, "I know teeth."

40

DDS

* * *

I wasn't about to mark time in another slow-motion taxi. Our colleagues at Impervious scrambled on my request for a rapid turnaround and I reserved their security services for the rest of the weekend. Valeriy Bubka made Roscoe discard his last bite of cream Danish before he let him load himself into the armored Range Rover. He dropped us off at the medical office tower on Park Avenue and waited on the street below.

On the afternoon of July 3rd, the towering office building was nearly empty. A solitary security guard managed to keep busy by scanning the screens in a circular plaza of monitors that surrounded her station in the foyer.

The view from the 40th floor of the building displayed the city's intensity from the Hudson to the East River and from the Empire State Building to Harlem. On the Friday afternoon before Saturday the Fourth, the doc's skeleton crew was reduced to him, a dental assistant and a hot-looking hygienist in her tight blue jeans.

An Afghanistan Tricare Dental Program Overseas plaque inside the doctor's office showed that he served as a Tricare OCONUS Preferred Dentist at the same time I was there. I never met him but it turned out we knew a lot of the same people and the same inside jokes. A few minutes after we met, Dr. Jorgenson quietly released his reduced workforce for the holiday weekend.

I assured him that this was a matter of the highest national security and not to worry about reprisals from *Herr* Keitel. Based on what I knew, Daddy Warbucks wouldn't be getting out of the country, even with his state-sanctioned Diplomatic Immunity.

When I mentioned my White House top-secret security clearance, Dr. Jorgenson raised an eyebrow and listened. When I couldn't provide my Triad or any other form of top-secret substantiation, his mouth turned down with suspicion. So, being on F.L.O.T.U.S. furlough, I called "FLOTUS" and hoped that Electra was quick on the uptake.

I spoke quickly: "Hello, Mrs. Jackson. Nick Wolfe. I'm sorry to interrupt but this is vital."

On the other end, my wife said, "Nick, this isn't Yvonne. You called me by mistake."

"I know, ma'am. I know. I need your help here. Because my Triad got smashed I don't have proof of my White House security clearance."

"Nick," she said, "I don't know what game you're playing, but this really isn't funny."

"Yes, ma'am. You're right. This is deadly serious. Dr. Anderson Jorgenson needs to see my authentication before he helps us save the president. But I haven't received my replacement Triad with my security clearances yet." I held on and waited. The three second silence felt like three hours.

In a reluctant *Mom* voice, she said, "Put him on."

I thought I contained my pleasant surprise rather well when I handed my phone to the dentist. He listened for a moment, nodded. Then he listened some more, nodded again. He gave a slight chuckle, handed it back to me.

I said, "Thank you, ma'am. I'll debrief later," and hung up.

The doctor eyed me with a whimsical expression in his eyes. I asked, "What?"

He said, "If that was the First Lady then I'm SpongeBob SquarePants. My nine-year-old boy plays hooky better than that. She said I should make a deal for your watch."

It didn't matter to him who the lady on the phone was. He knew a lot about who I was and about my recent headline grabbing exploits at the Birknerhaus Group, the Texas border, and about the medal I failed to receive. I should have led with those.

Doctor Jorgenson merely regarded Keitel as a Swiss banker with a lot of money. When I revealed why we were so insistent on grilling the man who oversaw funding for terrorist attacks and assassinations, his patriotism came alive. But he agreed with First Lady Electra Wolfe. He wanted my watch.

Like most Special Forces ops, the hunk of gold on my wrist served as emergency currency for a last-ditch measure to get me out of any country, any time, in the most dire circumstances. My personal Rolex Daytona "Eye of the Tiger" that departed on the doctor's wrist made sure he would never be late for another golf foursome. At much more than six figures, it was a high price to pay for the syringe and empty office he provided, but I figured it was worth it. I billed it to F.L.O.T.U.S., but I had an idea why Electra offered it in the deal.

Rudolf Keitel was already in the chair, high on nitrous oxide and benzodiazepines. Roscoe and I came into the room beneath our freshly donned smocks and masks. Despite our dental practice garb, the CEO of the central bank that oversaw all sovereign central banks recognized the Purple People Eater that stood beside me.

He spoke with surprise in his octogenarian Swiss accent. "*Herr* Ritter!" he said. "Is the delightful Miss Cocks with you? I spoke with Ariane–that welcher's sister." The laughing gas made him snigger much louder than he ever would have done in normal life.

The old guy reached for Roscoe's wrist, gripped it in his hand and spoke as best he could under the influence. "She was so angry!" He laughed out loud. "Your money will arrive soon, with interest. I made him include a case of *Chateau Lafitte*."

The jovial mastermind of murders laughed more and added, "We had good times, *ja*? That was fun! Please win more so I can do that again." He turned his head and examined my face. "And who is this new friend?" he asked.

A few minutes later he knew who I was. While he was in such a good mood, Roscoe helped me maneuver him into position. At first I wondered if I was doing the right thing. He seemed like an affable, benign old coot as he watched me. I drew the scopolamine hydrobromide from its glass vial, down through a crooked needle and into a syringe.

It wasn't easy delivering the truth tonic into the base of his spinal column, but I was motivated. For half an hour afterward, I almost felt bad for the man. Convulsions wracked his body in the chair. At his age, I hoped he lived long enough to talk.

* * *

When he ceased thrashing about and settled down, Rudolf Keitel knew who a lot of people were. He knew the payola people in the former White House, the traitorous leakers in government departments, and the phony Non-Governmental Agencies that drained American cash.

It was the second time I administered the truth serum to someone; it was the first time anyone laughed. Apparently *Herr* Keitel's body chemistry agreed with N2O. It produced lasting effects and he snickered as he spilled what he knew as if he pontificated to a class of fifth graders.

Yes, they financed failed assassination attempt *numero uno*. Yes, they were behind failed attempt *numero two-oh*. But they were tired of playing around. Those failures were attended to with maximum prejudice; fresh bodies for the hogs.

For this contract killing, on this national holiday, in this global setting, there was no room for error. They brought in the best. Results were guaranteed. It's why he came to New York.

Roscoe let out a low whistle. "Results, guaranteed. Hell, Nick. Whoever this guy is, he's reading your playbook."

I was losing my patience. "Who's pulling the trigger? What are they doing? Where? When?"

Keitel's head rolled from side to side when he answered. "Details." He scoffed. "I care little for details. I care only for results. 'Is he dead?' and, 'Yes, he is dead.' That is what I care about. Those are details for others to manage." He felt the effects of his nitrous oxide again and laughed out loud.

"The triggerman is one detail. One! You have no idea the number of details I deal with every day. My *untergeordneten* attend to details. If they fail, I attend to them. I attended to them after Pennsylvania, and I attended to them after Miami. If they fail again, I will do the same. I don't care.

"You Americans think you're special. It's *your* money we use," he said with a laugh, "and *your* weapons. Everything traces back to you, to your country." He laughed some more. "You Neanderthals. Your country finances all the terrorism in the world!"

Roscoe and I exchanged curious looks.

"Ach!" he said. "I doubt you would understand if I diagramed it for you on a chalkboard."

We maintained our closed lips and let him talk.

41

USA-AID

* * *

Through his snaggled teeth and missing incisors, the old bald Swiss gave us a classroom lecture on global terrorism and finance.

"The U.S. sends us billions of dollars as foreign aid through your USA-AID agency to our shell organizations around the world. We send your money back to one of our foundations, excuse me, one of *your* foundations of course, in the U.S.A. Then, that foundation donates it to a non-governmental organization. You call them NGOs; they have meaningless names like, "The Party for People's Rights and Liberation" or some such nonsense. Then that group donates to protests, riots, caravans, political campaigns."

Roscoe let out a quiet, low whistle. He whispered, "That's the biggest money laundering scam I've ever heard of."

Keitel continued, "Who do you think buys the tents and signs for agitators; T-shirts, clothes, food and water for the caravans across your border, and gets sympathetic stories broadcast in your national media?" He laughed again. "We use your own money to buy your judges, district attorneys, congressmen, senators, anyone we need."

"Senators? You can buy a United States senator?"

"Cheap!" he said, showing the influence of the laughing gas. "I can buy a senator for $20,000. You just caught one of yours hiding the gold bars we paid him with." He paused, rolled his eyes upward as he rolled his head. "What a simpleton. He tried to hide them in his suit. But this assassin!" he said. "That contract cost five million Swiss Francs." He looked over at Roscoe and laughed. "That's a lot of gold."

"But you don't know who he is?" My patience was shot. After everything, the shooting, the torture, the explosion of my home, POTUS, FLOTUS, Jack's briefcase, meeting with Mr. Allison–I wasn't ahead at all.

So, Keitel was the big money backer, but he only saw the view from 50,000 feet. His primary focus was on the central banks of 62 sovereign nations throughout Europe, Asia, South America, North America, Africa, and Oceania. Ground level details like Who and How were beneath his lofty vision. And I didn't have time to chase down a gaggle of middle managers. I popped the snap on my cross-draw holster. My double-barreled El Diablo filled my hand. I snarled, "I'm tired of screwing around."

I shoved a teeth spreader into his mouth and inserted the side-by-side derringer between his uppers and lowers. His eyes grew wider than its 12-gauge barrels. I growled, "You're big with money, Rudy. Let's talk about the most valuable commodity on earth. Lead."

If he didn't stroke out from the scopolamine, he might have from the twin steel breathing tubes I inserted into his mouth. I didn't care. We were running out of time and if he croaked, I considered it collateral damage.

I said, "Lead is the ultimate negotiator. You've got gold? I've got lead. You've got land? I've got lead. Both times, I win. Because it's lead that signs the bottom line in the ways of the world. So, here's my bottom line, Keitel. You have information, but I'm the one with the lead. It's going down tomorrow. Who, and how?"

I partially slid the gun out of his mouth so he had room to speak. He didn't. He eyed the gaping shotgun barrels and pissed his pants. *The doc isn't going to like that.* Then, through his missing number seven and ten lateral incisors and the rest of his yellow and gray misshapen teeth, around the barrels of my gun, he drooled out the corners of his mouth and down his chin.

I cocked the hammer back.

Roscoe grabbed my wrist. "He doesn't know, Nick! He told us what he knows. He's an asshole, but if you blow his head off, we'll have all kinds of crap to clean up, and I don't just mean gray matter."

I closed my eyes. My jaws were clenched so tight I expected to taste my fillings. My lips were compressed and I exhaled though my nose. I let out a deep breath, dropped the hammer of my pistol with a reluctant, slow release of my thumb. Roscoe earned his extra percentage point on our deal that day. I killed a lot of bad men, but I never murdered anyone.

*   *   *

We filled the banker with enough benzodiazepine in an IV to keep him asleep overnight. And he wouldn't wake up in his locked custodial closet alone. His pair of muscled-up eurotrash bodyguards were unconscious with him. Roscoe's immense girth, combined with his florid suit and surplus oversized teeth, served as irresistible distractions we employed to our benefit when I took them out.

When the happy trio regained consciousness on Saturday of the national holiday weekend, they could scream and pound all they wanted. Without their phones, nobody would hear them behind the lock and deadbolt of their 40th-floor storeroom until Monday morning. And Keitel wouldn't remember a thing that happened before he woke up in the dark with the mops and brooms. After we piled them into the darkness inside and locked the door, I stood with my hands in my pockets and studied the deadbolt lock. I hoped it held fast.

Roscoe's impish side came out when he revealed an old trick of his that was new to me. From his pants pocket, he jingled half a handful of coinage and said, "They'll never get out unless someone out here helps them."

He sat on the floor with his back against the wall on the opposite side of the corridor from the closet door. He pushed the soles of his shoes flat against it as high on the door as he could while still exerting leverage. "When I push hard and expand the gap in the doorjamb, slide a stack of pennies between the door and doorframe near the lock."

I inserted a stack of three pennies, then added more three-penny stacks of shims up and down the length of the doorframe. We retraced and expanded each point to four, then five pennies. The pressure exerted on the door and door jamb by the expansion of their space was so great Hercules couldn't turn the handle or work the lock. The pennies had to be chipped out first, from the outside.

Roscoe giggled like he probably did when he pulled this stunt in his old college dorm. He jingled some change in his hand and commented as we left, "And they want to stop minting these things."

I had things on my mind far beyond Rudy and The Closet Boys. We had a big day coming up. It was the USA's sestercentennial. And the President was going to be assassinated.

42

Liberty

* * *

E lectra couldn't hide the frustration in her voice when I called about our European trip's cancellation. I thanked her for tap dancing with Doctor Jorgenson on the phone with no advance warning. I tried to divert her attention with the good news that our family was home together for the holiday's festivities. When I explained how Roscoe helped and we got what we could from Keitel, her response was, "Oh. Working alone again, I see." *Mental note: pick up some yellow roses going back to the hotel. And pralines. She loves pralines. Where the Hell am I going to find yellow roses and pralines in Manhattan on July 3rd?*

A minute later I spoke with FLOTUS on my secured satellite phone, thanked her for including Donna in our family's group at the speech. She went straight to the point with her question.

I shot fast and straight. I told her I met with Mr. Allison, told her we agreed, told her about the evidence that the mastermind was at the top of the global financial pyramid, told her I got to him and told her the sincerity serum from Mr. Allison made him come clean about Pennsylvania, Miami and the whole international money laundering scam, with Roscoe as a witness.

And I told her the net result. We were in the same place we were before. Keitel was the boss of bosses who set the plans in motion. He knew What, When, Where and Why, but he didn't know Who or How, because he didn't care. It was his idea was to take out President Jackson and traumatize the USA on its biggest day. The setting and timing were his points of emphasis. As long as the job got done, What was the only thing important to him.

She asked who Roscoe was. Then, why did I bring him into it? How trustworthy was he? "He's the only reason we got to Keitel," I said. I was getting tired of the second-guessing. "And, he kept me from committing murder in the dentist's chair." I concluded that the best I could do was to be on site the next day, alert and ready to quick draw, whatever happened. I would see her Saturday on Liberty Island. *Hasta manana, baby.* I thought, *Here I go again, hip shooting on intuition.*

* * *

At high noon on Saturday, the Fourth of July, our Wolfe family boarded the *Carte Blanche II,* accompanied by my Gal Friday. Hotel management kept the mega-yacht reserved for guests of the *Maison Blanche,* moored at the city's super yacht harbor, North Cove Marina at Brookfield Place.

Electra's luxurious cruiser was available so hotel guests could enjoy the Circle Line sightseeing route around Manhattan Island without going to Midtown and Pier 83 in Hell's Kitchen. The boat was also outfitted for parties, light fishing, snorkeling, even SCUBA diving and underwater fish hunting for qualified divers. Everything needed to spend a day at sea with full crew and staff service was available on board. Rods, tackle, gaffs, nets, flippers, snorkels, masks, tanks and more could be had on request. Most often, "more" meant stiff drinks.

The Amer 100 that was named the *Carte Blanche II* was delivered out of Monaco and represented the most sophisticated nautical design. The yacht was solid white, in keeping with the late Preston T.'s motif and featured the highest Italian custom style and sumptuousness. 100 feet long, her beam was over 22 feet wide, created to provide total comfort to cruise in luxury for months.

Donna indulged herself in the opulence of the craft and I had fun watching her. She gently bounced on the white leather sofas in the main cabin, sat at the bar with a cocktail and drank in the rich Italian extravagance.

Captain Dan looked tough. Beneath a skipper's hat that lost its whiteness years ago, the skin of his forehead was wrinkled into a leathered texture, creased by years of salt and spray as a captain in the Merchant Marine. His broken ruddy nose above chapped lips belied his age of only 54 years. The twin 1,925 horsepower engines gurgled and burbled their nautical soundtrack as he backed us out of the harbor.

A man of few words, Captain Dan merited a good deal and a good life. He earned excellent pay and benefits, with room and board provided for him as the full time resident on the luxury superyacht. The grizzled old salt lived in the captain's stateroom and oversaw any necessary maintenance and upkeep with a small crew.

He piloted us into the channel of the Hudson River. We headed south between the populations on two shores and hundreds of boats that were caught up in the media frenzy of the national holiday event. Every hotel room in the city and surrounding area was booked by press from around the world. Each newspaper, radio network and online service showed a presence everywhere a person turned. And each TV news team brought a panel of a dozen commentators to tear apart every word in President Jackson's speech.

We motored from the marina in Battery Park straight south past Ellis Island, amid and through more than 100 Coast Guard launches that patrolled New York Harbor. They closed the port to commercial traffic for the day, directed traffic and provided security. Ahead of us, and in full view of every boat on the glistening water that day, stood one of the world's most recognizable icons.

43

Statuesque

*   *   *

I marveled in silence. Her lovely features basked with resplendence in the summer sun. She stood with proud strength as she looked out above the water and let the waves of the Hudson slip past. After I marveled at the elegant lines of the love of my life, I turned my gaze away from Electra standing at the bow's railing of the boat and beheld our nation's international symbol of freedom.

France first offered Frédéric Auguste Bartholdi's Statue of Liberty to Egypt to stand at Port Said. But when the land of the pyramids could not afford her price, she was regifted to the USA. In 1885 we didn't have enough money either, but Joseph Pulitzer of the *New York World* led a fund-raising campaign and amassed the needed capital from the American public. I always considered it Pulitzer's biggest prize.

After she was delivered in 214 crates to New York City, 20 men worked seven days a week to put her together. The completed construction in October 1886 resulted in her finished height of 151' 1" from the bottom of her base to the top of her gold-plated torch. Her iconic green color formed over a period of three decades on the thin sheet of copper, overlaid over what was originally the world's largest iron structure.

Miss Liberty rose with statuesque majesty above the masts and sails of hundreds of ships. Some of the authorized private craft were moored at the Ferry Terminal on the west side of Liberty Island. We drew near and pulled up at our reserved berth on the northeast boat dock. Some of our mooring neighbors were a pair of Chris-Craft motor yachts and a blue Scarab speedboat. Since I was a boy I have loved Scarabs. As we walked past, I sneaked looks at her from behind my shades like she was a bikini-clad surfer girl.

Usually, and especially on the Fourth of July, Liberty Island was packed with tourists. Not that day. The Secret Service controlled the admission of guests and press at their points of debarkation on the docks. And their list was tighter than a Scotsman's wallet.

The FBI ran an advanced background check on every invited guest. Dockside on Liberty Island, each individual was verified against the Secret Service's approved list, then scanned by agents with magnetometers and x-rays. On that historic day, no 25-dollar Crown Tickets were allowed so nobody looked out over New York Harbor through one of the elevated 25 windows in her crown. No public tickets were accepted at all, and of those who were allowed on the island, nobody went inside the statue. Guards and bomb-sniffing dogs patrolled the Lady's entrances and inner iron work.

And they seized my guns. Without my Triad I had no White House Top Secret security clearance. I was just a New York P.I. who presented my paperwork for my permit to carry in the city. They removed them anyway. *Feds.* Donna presented her pistol paperwork for the city. They seized her .38 snubby as well.

I was upset, but I understood. Actually, I was very upset. I felt hamstrung. I thought, *Am I being set up for something? Why did FLOTUS take me off of F.L.O.T.U.S.? Of all times, now? Who is and isn't armed here? There's nothing I can do about it. The Secret Service holds all the cards in this game and they can deal them any way they want.*

This really was The Big Lockdown. As Mr. Allison predicted, the Chief Executive's security was ubiquitous. I saw the Navy's Anti-Submarine Warfare surveillance boats that cruised on the surface with the Coast Guard, while Blackhawk helicopters provided surveillance and armament from the air. I could only believe with confidence that the F-35s patrolled at their lofty altitudes and high speeds.

A Harbor Police boat was moored far away from us at the end of the dock. Park Police, local cops, and Sheriff's deputies from two states provided highly visible pedestrian safety everywhere on the island.

As I walked with Electra and the boys, I verified my suspicions about the difficulties a sniper faced. The closest and best shooting locations were definitely unfeasible shots, behind the massive 27,000 ton concrete base of the statue. The presidential podium's Great Seal faced northeast, toward Whitehall and New York City. POTUS would look over and past the celebrating partiers in the crowd below, and the boat docking pier with the *Carte Blanche II*.

In 1976, to celebrate our bicentennial anniversary, Operation Sail featured 225 schooners, sloops, barques, barquentines, brigantines, ketches and yawls from 30 nations that participated in the New York Harbor parade. For the sestercentennial 50 years later, more than a hundred ships from 50 nations joined the honorary flotilla at Gravesend Bay just below the Verrazzano-Narrows Bridge.

Over 7,000 spectator boats and 60 naval vessels from a score of nations lined the route. On the shores of two states, more than 6,000,000 people watched from apartments, offices, rooftops, piers and in the parks.

They sailed 20 miles north up the Hudson toward the Bronx. Miss Liberty faced southeast and greeted them as she had so many incoming ships over the decades. But on that bright, historic summer day in American history, President Jackson wanted his address to be aimed toward the people of America from one of the 11 points of the star that made up her concrete base.

As we approached our grandstand seats, I examined the president's A-12 level multi-layered ballistic glass protection. It was crystal clear, almost invisible, and would defeat even the most perfect shot from the most powerful rifle. Any pistol bullet would stop like a slingshot marble against an armored truck.

Our VIP seats were literally on stage to one side of the president. On each wing of the platform, five rows held dozens of mega donors, family and friends within a few feet of POTUS.

I parked my butt in my assigned seat: north side stands, second row, aisle. Electra, Little Nick and Horace sat inside me, with Donna in the middle of the stands. Little Nick made Horace trade seats with him so he could make time with his new crush, my Gal Friday.

A moment after we settled in, the entertainment arrived.

44

Ham-hocks

* * *

To be sure, plenty of Beautiful People were on hand to be seen in the high-profile visibility on stage. The prestigious seating provided a convenient way for the president to register his appreciation to big money donors and corporations.

On that historic day, the people-watching scene exhibited an outer expression of the inner feelings of America. The president's supportive spectators represented the diversity of our people, ranging from corporate boardrooms, to celebrities, to costumes from the *Let's Make a Deal* game show.

They, or I should say we, were dressed in suits and ties for business meetings, shorts and T-shirts for a company picnic, and colorful costumes of American heroes.

My stunning wife was outfitted for the covers of New York's glamor sections. Subtle strips of red, white, and blue outlined the sleeves and pant legs of her thinly zippered cat suit. Its summer white fabric stretched against every curve of her body and was tucked inside her trademark high western boots.

Electra must have reached down and looked deep inside when she found whatever reason she picked me to marry. My surface level wasn't anything to write home about. I looked the same as usual: a five o'clock shadow despite shaving that morning, chinos, black polo shirt and mountain boots.

And Donna? Those painted-on white denim jeans and open-toed heels emphasized every step of the Donna Walk. Her Mets Jersey matched her orange and blue sunglasses and was untucked, tied together in a knot beneath cleavage that shimmered with SPF spray. My younger stepson in his Captain America T-shirt approved. That was the day his baseball team loyalties changed.

I did not want to say that the woman who waddled toward our grandstands was fat. It was pointed out to me in my ripe young forties that I needed to be more considerate of the values and points of view of others. But her extreme obesity class three BMI had to be over 45 and she tip-toed in heels like one of the hippos in *Fantasia*.

The guy she dragged in tow was distracting enough in his bright patriotic costume. He celebrated the occasion in red, white and blue American flag formal tails, with a matching Uncle Sam topper. In the July afternoon sunshine, thick perspiration formed on his brow. Rivulets of sweat streaked trails down his face makeup from beneath his white wig and dripped from under his fake beard.

Despite his vivid patriotic attire, his day-date managed to upstage him. The gravitational pull of her presence commanded the curiosity of every person present, along with several news cameras.

Her star-spangled eye glitter was visible from ten yards away and the brassy tinge on her over-bleached hairstyle provided us with a discordant complement to Miss Liberty's oxidized exterior. Her tortured high-heeled shoes buckled under the substantial mass of her *Ham-hocks Espanol.*

The bargain basement knockoff number she squeezed into resembled the yellow mini dress that Avalon modeled three days earlier on the street. Except for a couple of details that I couldn't call "small." Its shell of stitched and shiny patchwork vinyl pieces was several sizes logarithmically larger than the French model's smooth and sensuous Italian leather, and the needlework seams around her thick thighs and bulbous butt strained not to burst.

The couple took their seats in the grandstand at the end of the row in front of us. Behind the cover of my aviators, I noticed I wasn't the only man, woman, or child who worked to avert their eyes from the visual gravitational pull directed at us by the overpowering pair in the grandstand.

* * *

Nothing ever starts on time. Fortunately, the awning over our seats provided shade from the sun. The first speaker introduced the introductory speaker, who introduced the vice president's introductory speaker, who introduced the vice president, who spoke then stepped aside for the president. The crowd cheered.

As his favorite popular theme song played, John Jackson emerged and waved, smiling and shaking hands as he walked along the platform. After he crossed the stage a couple of times and gladhanded supporters, he addressed the podium to the strains of "Hail to the Chief." The big moment arrived.

He leaned forward into the microphone, paused a moment for effect. Then in his deepest, most reverential and presidential voice he declared, "My fellow Americans. Today–is a great day for America!"

Five yards to the president's left and ten feet from me, the big ball of overwhelming sunshine shot up from her seat. She crammed a little finger into each corner of her mouth. The wolf-whistle blast that shrieked from between her lips must have been heard as far away as Car-Jack-Is-Stan.

Every news channel camera zoomed in on her for a close up. Her escort hid his face inside his stars and stripes top hat. Electra subtly turned to me and in a catty voice I've only heard outside of ladies rooms on party nights, said with a sarcastic lilt, "Just think, that could be you right now." Then, to add a one-word rim-shot for extra comic effect, she leaned in and whispered an additional dig into my ear in a melodramatic mock-sexy voice.

I was stunned. That was it, the jigsaw puzzle solution.

The last word she said was the answer to the clue I was straining to identify. It was the expression I struggled to pull out of my groggy mind, the one that stood out in the background of my drunken whiskey-boarding session. All the pieces that flew around in a turbulent cyclone within my head crashed together in a cataclysmic revelation. That one word was the cornerstone. It acted like a powerful electromagnet and pulled them all together where they formed an instant flawless picture.

I bolted from my aisle seat, bounded down the two rows of grandstands below me and sprinted across the concrete base, away from POTUS and his podium. The standing crowd full of startled and curious faces parted as I charged through them. A pair of gray-flannelled Secret Service agents ran after me, but I had a flying start ahead of them. I hit a stride and left them fading behind.

The crowd gasped. Behind me, I heard President Jackson comment, "Who's that? Is that Nick Wolfe again?" He said with a laugh, "I'm telling you folks, that guy will do anything to upstage me."

It was a long drop, but I hung over the edge of the northeast star point and released myself to the ground below. Paint buckets and construction materials created an obstacle course between me and the dock.

As I ran through and past the piles of junk, the gallery of patriotic partiers I left behind broke into a collective stress-relieving laugh. It began with uncertainty, then gained reassurance among the rank and file and grew into a roar, prompted by President John Jackson's comments.

I dashed toward the dock and heard his amplified voice call again from behind me. "Nick, if you're going to streak, you're supposed to wear your birthday suit!" The multitudes clapped with raucous laughter. "And it's our nation's birthday, not yours!"

As I sprinted away from them toward the water, the crowd's amusement grew into applause and chants of, "USA! USA! USA!" A National Park Police officer stood directly ahead of me in my pathway to the dock. His initial intent was to block and tackle me with widespread arms and legs–until he looked up at the president.

Over my shoulder and behind me, he saw that President Jackson continued to make a joke of it and people went along with his quips and laughed with him. "Nick, come back," he called. "We're going to have fireworks and hot dogs!"

The merriment and applause grew and the officer shrugged with a confused smile as I tore past him. I sprinted onto the dock and made an instant analysis of my available transports at hand.

Far ahead of me, Captain Dan leaned his long, tan limbs on the shining chrome rails of the *Carte Blanche II* cigarette deck. He watched me with nonchalance and an eyebrow raised in curiosity as I ran toward him down the dock. When I reached his boat he looked down, flicked his cigarette away in a beautiful end-over-end geometric arc that kissed the water with a hiss.

Electra's mega-yacht was not an option. Her hull speed in open water was awesome, but she was too slow to start up, back out, get going and get up to speed. Especially for a short all-out sprint through a hundred sailboats and oilers that tried to avoid crashing into each other. By the time I had backed her away from the dock, I could have landed in a faster, more nimble launch.

I looked up at Captain Dan. "I need the fastest boat here!"

45

Aces

*   *   *

Nonplused, the skipper turned. He elevated his vision by lifting his head, surveyed the boats lined up along the pier. In an instant, he pointed with a gnarled index finger toward the far end.

I ran in the direction of his choice, dashed past the beautiful blue Scarab. *Damn. I always wanted to pilot a Scarab.* The pair of Chris-Craft motor yachts lounged in the water beside each other like a pair of old drinking buddies in their floating chairs with beers. I stopped and looked back.

The tall, lean figure jabbed the air with his finger and pointed farther down the dock. The boat he indicated floated at the end, near the Harbor Police boat. The seventies-era drag boat sat flat and low in the water, like a crocodile about to spring at its next meal and almost invisible among the other sea craft.

Her massive engine rose up in the air with a pair of gaping exhaust pipes that reached even higher. Rays of light reflected up off the water that lapped against her sides and made her chrome velocity stacks gleam in the bright sunlight. I dropped down from the dock and landed on top of her glossy black aircraft paint.

Between my boots atop the deck of the 19-foot Peterson, the painting of a skeleton in a derby hat smoked a fat blunt and grinned. His bony fingers clutched a poker hand of four aces and the king of diamonds. Gold leaf paint atop the aircraft black proclaimed the speedboat's name: *ACES HIGH*.

I dropped down into the pilot's seat of red metalflake vinyl. No key. It was a car engine; a big one, a powerful one. But nevertheless, a 711 CID twin-turbo hemi engine was still a car engine. And I still knew how to hotwire.

Seconds later, I blasted the massive engine to life. *ACES HIGH* was parallel parked at the dock's end, so I cast off, slammed the throttle forward and blew the engine's carbon out of its massive exhausts. I rooster-tailed away from the massive event and roared across the short seaway toward the southern corner of Ellis Island.

The puzzle pieces continued to swirl in my head, but this time I saw the picture that they formed. I knew What, When, Where, Why, plus How–and Who*m*. The loose pieces in my mind attached together into one big mosaic of disaster:

> *Jack*
> *Briefcase*
> *weapons hijacked*

Ukraine
your money
your weapons
your president
in front of the entire world
sniper distances
bulletproof glass
Athens
Videos
Milan
fashion shows
Paris
runways
"fashion backward"
photo shoots
photo pinups
Jack's office
The Park
Jack's pawn ticket
"tag with you"
Sol murdered
Marseille

The puzzle pieces that whirled in a tempest of information overload stopped. They clacked together like a hundred earth magnets and formed one big clear jigsaw puzzle picture. It was a portrayal of indescribable beauty in a picture of death. When

Electra spoke into my ear, she said the magic word that opened Ali Baba's cave. "Just think, that could be you right now, *Dah-ling*."

Thicker than any regatta lineup, a motley armada of nautical revelers blocked my route. Tall sailing ships muddled about in irons among luxury mega-yachts that dwarfed the *Carte Blanche II*. Charter fishing boats cruised among small motorboats, even kayaks.

Those were the civilians. The Coast Guard, Harbor Police and U.S. Navy were present with their security forces as well. I didn't care. I didn't have a second to spare. I slammed the throttle forward and made the speedboat's engine scream.

Marine air horns shrieked at me as I cut and swerved between the sailboats and the oilers. People yelled and waved their arms. A committee boat for yacht racing fired its race-finish cannon at me.

My mind didn't think. My gut said, "No time for Mr. Nice Guy."

From island to island, I shot in and out among the shouting protestations and horn blasts of offended maritime Americans on their summer holiday booze barges. When I pulled up at the end of my short sprint, the pieces to the puzzle that plagued me still formed the same stunning, gorgeous image of evil.

I saw it all in my mind's eye: *They weren't going to shoot him with a gun. They couldn't shoot him with a gun. They couldn't attack from land, air or water. Holy Hell. Ukraine. Hijacked. They were going to ...*

On Ellis Island, the north side housed a national immigration museum. The southern side was closed to the public. Only scheduled private tours of the former Ellis Island Immigrant Hospital were permitted. On the southeast corner of the island nearest the Statue of Liberty, the former staff house number 17 stood open, vacant, available, forgotten.

They wouldn't have been successful with any sniper rifle, but that wasn't what they intended to use. The shooting distance of 1,300 yards was well within the range of what they hijacked from our military weapons shipment to Ukraine.

A thick, vivid white concrete curb surrounded the island and there was no place to dock. I roared up to it, leapt off the boat and let it drift. A short sidewalk half overgrown with grass led to the entrance of the old staff housing building. Before I reached it, a 6'1" Amazon stepped outside through the door.

*　　*　　*

Senta left her chauffeur livery outfit at home. Dressed for the occasion, she stayed with her motif of ballistic black with shiny zippers in a stretch fabric one piece suit. And boots.

Are those savate boots? Who the Hell wears savate boots?

With a strong German accent, she said, "It is unfortunate you are here, *Herr* Wolfe. We planned fun things for the three of us."

I said, "What's going on, Senta?"

She said, "Go inside and see. If you can."

Inside my head, I chuckled with confidence: *Don't tempt me, baby. I'm in no mood for bimbo-fu.* "Get out of my way," I said. "I'm going in."

She replied with a smirk on her lips, "You should have come inside Monday, *Mein Herr.* Then, you would have enjoyed it. Today, I think not so much."

"Move," I said. I stepped toward her to shove her aside. She faked low to my leg before she landed a lightning strike with her foot on my left jaw that almost knocked me off my feet. The flat sole and rounded edge of her combat footwear was designed to strike with devastating blows.

Using the leverage of her yardstick inseams, she literally kicked like the proverbial mule. I was stunned, took a step back. But I shook it off and lunged ahead. Her next savate kick hammered into my right jaw.

The acrid tase of adrenaline filled my mouth. I thought, *OK, let's see you handle the bums rush of 6'4" and 243 pounds.* I charged to take her down. Whap! Before I took a second step, she kicked again–and broke my left jaw!

I would have used my Triad if I had it. *The Hell with it.* I didn't need the Triad's Meth-Adrenaline Delta 9. I was pissed off. I felt the supercharge of my own adrenaline surge through my body in response to the injury.

Her kick came at me again. This time, I intuitively reverted to the proprioception of my Delta training and regained my balance. I could predict more about how a human body was about to move than a kinesiologist. And I knew exactly what I was going to do next.

With my faculties under the influence of my supercharged adrenaline rush, her foot looked like it traveled so slowly that I marveled at the shape of her leg's elongated musculature beneath the tight black fabric. Her ankle traveled straight into the waiting crook of my left hand. I snatched it and locked it down in a grip that would crush rocks.

Savate boxers can kick and punch like Hell. They can *fouetté*, they can *chassé*, they can *coup de pied bas*, but they can't grapple worth a damn. I swept her back leg and took her down. When I leapt on her and put her neck into a triangle, her face registered anger, then panic as I squeezed tighter, then tighter.

Her desperate eyes tried to read my face, then strained to deny the grim mask of death they saw. She knew it was here; she knew it was now; she knew there wasn't a damn thing she could do about it. She said, "Kiss me," just before I, well, like I said, "No more Mr. Nice Guy."

Behind me, I heard horns blast and people yell. Another committee boat cannon report echoed across the water. I stood up.

My jaws hurt like Hell with a numb, enduring pain. Even Jet never hit me like that. I held my jaw together with my left hand as I slammed the building's door with my right shoulder and crashed through. Inside, I saw the picture that the pieces formed inside my head. I wished they were wrong, but the internationally famous top model stood before me as the target in my crosshairs.

46

Chiaroscuro

* * *

*T*he object of my vision cut through my thoughts and
invaded my feelings: My God, she's beautiful. That
hypnotic face, those penetrating eyes, that killer body. Gorgeous,
famous, beyond suspicion. Travels the world, wherever the hit's
going down. The perfect assassin; "just a sweet, pretty girl."

*Paris? No problem: the houses of Dior, Chanel, Lanvin, Hermes,
YSL and Givenchy are in the Golden Triangle. Milan? The
home of Prada, Gucci, Armani, and Dolce & Gabbana. New
York? "I live in NOHO, darling."*

*She makes a million bucks a shoot, and five million a shot. With
her sidekick, Senta—well, her former sidekick, Senta, the way they
look they could pull off anything; like hijacking a U.S. military
truck of Javelin missiles destined for Ukraine.*

And there they stood before me: a pair of FXM-148 Javelin
missiles on tripods. Each one was positioned at a window in
the southeast corner of the old building. In white grease pen,
one was arrogantly marked, "His" and the other, "Hers."

Javelins were the ideal weapons for this murderous mission, "fire-and-forget missiles." Their pre-launch target lock-on and automatic self-guidance to the unfortunate recipient made them an "aim 'em, fire 'em and forget about 'em" solution. Shoot, and scram. And each missile was aimed at Liberty Island: one for him, one for her.

Air cover? Water security? Underwater security? Secret Service? Police? Harbor Police? A-12 bulletproof glass? All useless. Javelin missiles soared 150 yards high, far above the tallest masts of any ships, then fired straight down and destroyed their targets.

Each missile used two shaped charges. Their flight profiles were designed to first strike the more vulnerable top armor of tanks. The first charge was a precursor that opened a hole in the top of the tank, followed by a primary warhead that devastated 46-ton war machines.

One Javelin would blow the president to Timbuktu; the other would topple Miss Liberty into the Hudson River like the Colossus of Rhodes. On the day of America's sestercentennial celebrations, the attack on American soil in the Big Apple would traumatize the nation as much as 9-11.

Straight ahead of me, Avalon stood in front of a window as she aimed her missile on its tripod. The old building was rough inside, dilapidated with no attempts at renovations. Ancient, stained acoustic ceiling tiles hung down, and paint peeled from the walls. At the crashing sound of my entrance through the door, she stood aside.

That day, she traveled incognito again. Her sensational body was cloaked within a loose-fitting light gray track suit with gray jogging shoes. She wore the jacket tied around her waist with the sleeves in a knot. A wide black belt of elastic stretched tight around her middle above a tight yellow Spandex jogging shirt. Her hair was put up inside a Yankees ball cap, with a pair of infrared-defeating shades snapped to her temples above its brim.

I said, "Hey, ugly duckling. Let's take a rain check on this one. I'll buy you a hot dog back at the park."

She was shocked at the sight of me. I had that effect on people. She stood aside, glanced at Senta's Javelin, looked over at hers, then back at me.

It hurt like Hell to mouth those few words through my swollen face and jaws. Though I held them in place, they didn't work well, and I sounded like I was full of Novocain. I wished I had some; the pain sapped my strength. I needed to kill her quickly before I succumbed to the physical distress I knew I was denying. I muttered through a thickened tongue and inoperable jaw. "Your comical sidekick ran out of kicks."

A flash of anger passed over her face, then vanished as quickly as it appeared. With standard sociopathic detachment, she said, "Quelle dommage. She wanted a menage a trois."

"I gave her le petit mort," I said.

Her hand slid behind the small of her back. In a flash, a glint flitted across the room. The knife sliced through my right bicep, stuck into the bone. Its sharp, vivid pain was almost a relief from the dull throbbing of my jaw.

It was on now. I reached with my left hand for the knife's handle to jerk it out and plunge it into her heart. All I wanted was to feel my fingers around that fair-skinned neck. And now I had her shiv.

The next dagger cut through my left quadricep and planted itself in my femur. I stopped dead in my tracks. I reached for the knife's handle, and the blade already in my hand clattered to the floor. I didn't want to stop; I couldn't stop. My right leg dragged my left behind it as I pulled myself toward her. There was no way she wasn't going to die.

Another knife. She's really good. My left bicep felt the blade pierce the muscle all the way through to the bone. Nice try, but nothing's going to stop me from killing you.

I could only feel pain in one spot at one time, but that spot was my whole body. I hurt everywhere at the same time. Inside my head, the back of my mind let out a pained, piercing scream. The next knife flew across the room, speared my right quad and stabbed into the bone. I hit the deck.

She looked down at me on the floor, then spoke in a mocking tone of voice. "Pauvre petite garcon," she said. "You are still upset. Lately, things just do not seem to go well for you."

In my mind, I grabbed her lithe physique with one hand and thrashed her up, down, and around like an empty trash bag. I reached forward, bit my fingernails into the linoleum through decades of dust and dirt. I tried to pull myself forward across the filthy floor but my strength was gone and I lost my grip. I couldn't look up at her. I lay on my side. I could think, but I couldn't feel anything.

"I weesh things are different, Nick. You and I; we are much alike. We would be—*magnifique*. Quite the couple."

I strained my neck and looked up. I said, "'Couple?' You crazy bitch. Zero plus 1 is 1. Because I'm going to kill you; and I work alone."

Avalon reached behind her back into her elastic belt and produced another deadly accessory. Sunlight glinted off the steel shaft of the icepick in her hand. She laughed, and in a sing-song voice said, "Au Revoir, Monsieur."

* * *

Suddenly, Avalon's eyes flew wide open. Her cobalt irises strained themselves in an aggrieved three-thousand-mile stare straight ahead. The shaft that shot across the empty space impaled her sternum and pinned her celebrated body back against the peeling wall paint. In slow disbelief, she looked down at the spear, turned her face up again and recognized the shooter. Then she laughed.

This time, the thin red trickle across her lips wasn't YSL *Rouge Pur Couture*. Her head dropped to her chest, her Yankee blue ball cap toppled to the concrete floor, and her platinum locks swayed back and forth for the last time.

More lifeblood saturated her tight jogging *chemise* around the penetration wound as the spot slowly spread its darkness outward and turned her yellow top brown. From my involuntary prone position on the floor, I looked up. I watched the pupils of her eyes as they flooded their blackness outward into her fading cobalt irises until her hypnotic lights were slowly, gradually, extinguished.

I choked, felt like I swallowed a frog. I felt the recoil inside my guts as they tried to heave up through my throat. My arms, my legs, nothing worked. I was immobile. But I was alive.

I couldn't straighten my legs due to the excruciating pain and curled into a fetal position on my side. I heard the sound of someone walking across the floor. I strained my neck again and looked up.

The dim and blurred picture I saw was the soft focus view of an avenging angel. She moved toward me in white, with a tall and lean curvaceous body, soft brown eyes, shagged auburn big hair, a face cosmetic surgeons would envy, and a little dimple in her chin.

I said, "Hello, Judge."

She walked over to me, rested the ostentatious yellow handle of her Cressi compressed gas speargun on the floor next to the toe of a white ostrich cowboy boot. Her flat tone of voice was devoid of humor. "Working alone again, I see."

I made one more try at deflection. "Your...chiaroscuro...needs work."

Then I heard the most feared words in the English language. "Nick," she said, "We need to talk."

47

Denouement

* * *

Two months and a liquid diet of soups and smoothies later, I looked as rough as usual but was able to speak without too much pain. My wired jaw and dental implants were new experiences, unlike the physical therapy and rehab work that got me walking again, albeit with the aid of a cane.

It wasn't like I never took a blow to the head before. Jet clocked me one day in the ring harder than I ever got hit in Afghanistan Close Quarters Battle. Even he didn't match the intense impact of Senta's savate kicks. I learned later how well trained and practiced she was, as well as the deadly nature of her supermodel partner in crime.

Earlier in May, Electra and I were married in the White House Rose Garden. This time, in October, I found myself there again, accompanied once more by the president, but not as my Best Man.

When the dust settled and I became presentable, our President and Commander in Chief awarded me the Congressional

Medal of Honor. Governor Stinson of Texas, as Commander in Chief of the Texas Army, plus the Joint Chiefs of Staff, officially recognized the rank of Lieutenant Colonel I received as a battlefield commission from Brigadier General Rhys Willoughby of the Texas Army at Alamo II.

President Jackson read these words: "In the name of the United States Congress, for conspicuous gallantry and intrepidity and the risk of life above and beyond the call of duty at Alamo II ..." The president read the official military summary and details of my work in Brackettville, Texas when we defeated the foreign invasion at the border.

Then he added a few more words of his own and placed the light blue ribbon with five white stars around my neck. As he spoke, I looked down and admired the Army's variant of the award, with its bronze star and the head of Minerva in the center, suspended from a bar bearing the word "Valor."

But he didn't leave it at that. After he reiterated the story behind my drunken fiasco on Madison Avenue and added jokes about my "streaking" at the Statue of Liberty, the President of the United States thanked me as the second Wolfe in our family who saved life.

Then the fun began.

* * *

On a rainy autumn weekday, Electra's honey-brown eyes focused on her fourth-floor chiaroscuro archery targets while

Little Nick and I played catch inside the White Mansion. We avoided the furnishings with our baseball inside the zeppelin hangar living room when the president's call came through. At the sound of his "Hail to the Chief" ring tone, I fumbled my phone with my outfield mitt to catch his call. "Want to join me for lunch?" he asked.

With her usual unexpected perfect timing, Electra appeared downstairs as I hung up the call. I wasn't crazy about my wife's persistent desire to be involved in my cases, but she had a way of making a concise and convincing closing argument.

"Don't ever tell me, 'I work alone' again," she said. "If I didn't get Captain Dan to break 50 maritime laws and blast across the Hudson behind you, there'd be an icepick in your back, the president would be dead, and the Statue of Liberty would be at the bottom of the Hudson."

The FBI had a lot more than just "files" on Avalon and Senta. At first, they said they didn't have anything. But after a whistleblower risked his life and livelihood and testified before Congress, they admitted they had them, but they were redacted. When the Attorney General ordered them anyway, the FBI replied that they were sealed for 65 years.

Electra joined us in the Beast when the Commander in Chief paid a personal unannounced visit down the street to the J. Edgar Hoover Building on Pennsylvania Avenue. With a full detail of Secret Service federal agents, and with both DOJ and

DHS Directors in attendance, he walked into the headquarters of the FBI and demanded to be handed the files.

In plain and simple language, he declared, "I am the Commander in Chief; I am the President of the United States; your director serves at my pleasure and I demand those complete unredacted files, now."

"I will leave this building with both of those assassins' files in hand, completely unredacted, or I will fire every single person that stands in my way until I get them. That will be without severance, without pension, and they will be charged with obstruction of justice by the Attorney General, who is here with me now to do just that, on the spot."

AVALON DU BOIS

was at the top of the food chain for hired guns. Runways and photo shoots around the world gave her an undeniable cover and access to world leaders, society parties, yachts, private jets. Athens, Paris, Milan, London, New York, Rio and Buenos Aires; all were high profile locations and fashion centers for runways and photo shoots.

The ugly duckling daughter of a French *Maréchal des logis-chef* in the French Foreign Legion, Avalon du Bois believed she was doomed to a life ahead of sneers and condescension because of her gangly body and awkward features. Well into her teens, she was the target of jokes from the kids and even older adults because of her gawky looks.

Her dossier did not go into her family background beyond her father, but it was obvious he taught her the Legion's *Combat de Contact Intense* or, "C4" in his 1st Foreign Cavalry Regiment, south of Marseille. So, she learned from her father, and she learned from his friends. They taught her CQB, taught her to shoot, taught her sniper skills. They taught her how not to be seen.

But they didn't teach her to be a murderer. Avalon achieved that distinction on her own with the help of the resident assassins for hire in Marseille. She practiced every lethal art she could, enjoyed her ability to achieve vengeance against the elites of society for looking down on her when she was young. To her, those childhood rejections and embarrassments were manifest in every victim she destroyed.

When her features matured and the swan bloomed from the ugly duckling at age 20, Avalon found a new avenue for her deadly calling: modeling. Her rapid ascension into higher social circles provided her with gracious entry to anywhere in the world: palaces, casinos, parties, businesses, halls of state.

Her fame gave her access to society's most elite figures. Everybody knew Avalon, and if they didn't, they didn't need to. They were stunned by her beauty. That access paid her more for her kills than her modeling gigs and photo shoots, and she enjoyed the work on a different, dark, level.

SENTA TINKIN

was an even more fascinating case. Avalon's sidekick served in Austria's version of Delta Force as a *Jagdkommando* lieutenant in Austria's 61st *Landwehrstammregiment* in *Kitzbühel*.

She was a *tireuse,* an expert in savate fighting, and served in the War in Afghanistan as part of ISAF/Resolute Support, but there was no way I would have known her. Her time was seven years after I left the theatre. After her military stint she hooked up with Avalon on a playful weekend in Istanbul. Her special forces tradecraft dovetailed perfectly with the runway assassin's and they moved in together as a team.

She dressed out at over six-feet tall and 155 pounds and with the leverage from those yardstick stems, it's no wonder my jaw was still tender months later. On the very lowest part of her abdomen, Senta's autopsy revealed a tattoo in gothic script. The *Jagdkommando* unit's motto is "*Numquam Retro*"–Latin for, "Never Retreat."

And speaking of partners in crime, while I was in Walter Reed Hospital, Electra and I scheduled a time to "talk of many things." That time was just around the corner. We agreed that on our next break, we would charter our honeymoon train again and ride cross-country to visit Trouble and Josh Hitt in Hollywoodland. I said that would make a good environment for long, uninterrupted talks about things. She agreed.

But her ten-year-old *consigliere*, little Nick, ambushed me: "So, what about your detective agency, *Peligro*? What about

Murgatroyd? What about Donna? She's hot! And Norm? He can help me with my computers! Are they coming to Washington with you? What about Cody? Can he play in the house? Can he sleep in my room?"

My wonderful wife, the woman whose quiet depth beneath still waters always knew what was going on and who arrived with impeccable timing whether it was with coffee, tea or a speargun, shrugged. Her look was a picture of feigned innocence as if to say, "Don't look at me."

I knew a pincer movement when I saw one. And I knew when I was outnumbered and outgunned. I needed to deploy emergency countermeasures. I fired off five words that have saved thousands of marriages: "Let's talk about it later."

Watch for Nick Wolfe's next adventure–COMING SOON!

Afterword

Thank you for reading Nick Wolfe's latest adventure. I hope you had fun and enjoyed the ride.

Please post a review on Amazon. It helps readers find this and other books by Indie authors.

The next Nick Wolfe adventure is already in the works!

In the meantime, if you enjoyed this Nick Wolfe thriller you might like others:

IMMIGRATION INVASION! *A Family Affair*

MAXIMUM PREJUDICE: *A Love Story*

"You may love it, you may hate it, but I guarantee you'll be entertained."

Your humble scribbler,

Robert